Love's Perfect Gift

A Novella

Jonita Mullins

Love's Perfect Gift

ISBN: 978-0-9789740-6-0

First Printing: November 2019

Cover photo by clarkcg photography
Used with permission

candleshine
publishing

Candleshine Publishing
Muskogee, Oklahoma
Printed in the U.S.A.

Dedicated to the people of my
hometown of Muskogee,
one of the friendliest towns
in the world.

Love's Perfect Gift

Chapter 1

The handsome cowboy crouched low in the saddle as his horse raced along the canyon rim. Behind him three angry desperados gained ground as their own horses churned up dust in the waning daylight. Glancing over his shoulder, the young cowpoke smiled confidently then spoke words of encouragement to his faithful steed.

In a moment his horse made a great leap and seemed to hang suspended in air. Slowly the words "To Be Continued" panned across the giant movie screen and the theater's audience groaned in a mixture of disappointment and anticipation.

Alex Barnett chuckled as the house lights came up and the theater goers – mostly kids from the local schools – stood to leave. He helped his pretty wife Laura slip into her coat and they also stepped out into the carpeted aisle of the Roxy Theater.

"We'll have to wait a whole week to see if Gene Autry survives that leap," he said over the excited chatter of the kids.

"Something tells me he'll be just fine," Laura smiled. The pretty brunette pulled a stocking cap over her hair and tied a brightly patterned cashmere scarf around her neck.

The young couple walked slowly toward the theater lobby allowing their fellow movie watchers to get ahead of them. Once outside they paused under the massive marquee which announced that Will Rogers would appear with his vaudeville act the following week.

Laura pulled on her gloves and Alex buttoned his coat against the cold. It was an overcast day in early December and there was a taste of snow in the air. If they received a snowfall, it would be the first of the season for Muskogee, a small town in Oklahoma that could get some significant snowfalls on occasion.

"Well, what shall we do now?" Alex asked. It was a rare Saturday when one or the other of the young newlyweds was not working and they planned to spend this day enjoying the time together.

Laura worked as a sales clerk at the perfume counter at Calhoun's Department Store and Alex worked at whatever odd jobs he could find after his classes at Bacone College. They had few funds for entertainment so the nickel tickets to a Saturday morning serial were a treat.

"Why don't we walk around downtown and look at the Christmas displays?" Laura suggested. "All the stores have outdone themselves this year. I think they're worried that it's going to be a slow Christmas shopping season."

It was a tradition for the shops along Broadway to put up elaborate window displays during the holiday season to entice shoppers to come inside. Laura had helped with Calhoun's display, working after hours with the other shop girls to fill the big display windows with beautifully wrapped packages. Marvin's Cycle Shop had an elaborate miniature train set running in its windows and Susman's Jewelry had a mechanical Santa that danced to music piped out to the sidewalk.

The couple left the theater and walked to Second Street, then turned north to arrive at Calhoun's, the largest downtown department store. They strolled slowly past it then moved on to other colorful window displays, pointing out the most expensive gifts and promising to give them to one another – someday.

They paused at McEntee's Jewelers where a dozen or more Swiss cuckoo clocks kept perfect time together. Noting that they were just a few minutes away from the top of the hour, they waited along with a few other shoppers for the cuckoo birds to make their appearance.

Nestled among the clocks were velvet-lined cases holding lovely pieces of jewelry. The gemstones sparkled through the thick leaded glass windows.

"Oh, look, Alex," Laura pointed to a set of heart-shaped silver earrings resting on black velvet in small square box. "Those match my grandmother's locket. Don't you think so?"

Alex bent down a little to study the silver pair. "Yeah," he agreed.

Laura looked at the earrings wistfully. "My grandmother told me she once had earrings to match the locket she gave me. But she had to sell them to pay medical bills when Grandpa came home from the war."

"The Great War?" Alex asked. Knowing the age of Laura's grandparents, that seemed unlikely.

"Laura smiled. "No, the Spanish-American War. Grandpa was a Rough Rider like a lot of other Muskogee boys. He came back home from Cuba with malaria. It took him a long time to get well and the medicine was expensive."

Alex studied the earrings more closely. "I think they have the same filigree pattern as your locket."

Laura disguised her smile by acting delighted with the sudden chorus of cuckoos that could be heard even through the thick glass. Not many men would notice filigree patterns, but her husband was an artist – a very talented artist – and he studied pattern and design wherever he found them.

While Laura watched the cuckoos, Alex studied the earrings, feeling certain they were the ones her grandmother must have sold. What a perfect Christmas gift they would make for Laura, but there was no price on the little jewelry box. Could he afford them?

He knew the answer – probably not. He was currently without a job and unless he found work or could sell his painting in the next month, there would be no way that he could purchase those earrings. And he knew Laura would never ask for them even though he could tell from the wistful look on her face that she would love to have them.

Laura took his hand and pulled him away from the display. "Come on," she said. "I want to see the mink coats at Graham's Department Store."

"Why?" Alex laughed. "It hardly gets cold enough here to need a mink."

"I know, but that won't keep Mother from expecting one. The wife of Sam Rigsby must keep up appearances, you know, even if she has to suffocate in a hot coat."

Laura's voice said she was jesting, but Alex thought he heard an edge of bitterness in it. Laura came from a wealthy home, but had given it all up to marry a poor art student who was years away from providing a decent living for them. She hadn't spoken to her parents since their wedding in June.

They crossed Broadway and walked to the smaller, more exclusive department store where the minks were displayed among glittering Christmas trees and fake snow. Laura studied the coats for a time then pointed to a rich, dark sable. "There," she smiled. "That's the one Mr. Graham will advise my father to buy for mother."

"Why that one?" Alex asked. "Is that her favorite style?"

"No," Laura shook her head. Her voice held a touch of irony. "That's the most expensive one."

"Oh," Alex said. "Of course."

Laura shook her head as if ridding it of a bad memory. "Let's go," she said and they left the mink coats behind. After they had walked both sides of Broadway, admiring all the displays and weaving around the many shoppers who lined the sidewalks Alex asked, "How about a cup of hot cocoa?"

"Sounds good to me," Laura smiled up at her handsome husband. "All this shopping has been exhausting."

Laughing the couple turned the corner at Third Street without either having to say where they would go for their refreshment on this cold Saturday. The Sugar Bowl Café was an artists' hangout and their favorite place to enjoy the rare treat of dining out.

They reached the door of the small café and saw a flyer advertising a poetry reading for the following week. The owner of the eatery, Miss Nettie Wheeler, was a great supporter of the arts and the various artists who lived in their small town. A testament to that were the numerous paintings that hung on every wall. An early watercolor that Alex had completed a few years ago also graced one wall. It was for sale, as were all the other paintings, baskets and sculptures, but so far few pieces had sold. There was little money in 1934 for such luxuries as artwork.

Alex and Laura found a table and removed their coats before taking their seats. After a server took their order, Alex looked around to see if any new paintings had been added, or if any might have sold.

"That landscape by Blue Eagle is gone," he noted, pointing to the spot the painting had once occupied. Blue Eagle was the name the artist signed on his paintings. His actual name was A.C. McIntosh and he was Alex's art teacher at the college.

"Oh, good; that was a favorite of mine," Laura said. "After yours, of course."

"You have to say that," Alex grinned as the waitress set their hot cocoa on the table. Generous dollops of whipped cream sprinkled with crushed peppermint candies made the beverage a nice treat.

"You sure you don't want the special today?" the girl asked. "It's Chub's famous meatloaf with a baked potato and his fluffy biscuits."

"No, this is fine, Susie" Laura smiled at young woman. "Thank you."

Neither felt a need to tell Susie they didn't have the money for the lunch special. An occasional cup of coffee or chocolate was about the only indulgence they could afford.

Susie nodded, and then moved on to other tables. They sipped their hot beverage in silence for a moment. Laura hoped Alex wasn't embarrassed that they couldn't buy lunch. She knew the lack of income hurt his pride.

"Professor McIntosh told the class the other day that there might be some jobs available soon for art projects through some new government program."

"Alex, that would be wonderful," Laura said. "What kind of projects?"

"Murals, I think. In public buildings like libraries, post offices, courthouses; things like that. He said he'd try to get all his students involved. He's working with Dr. Foreman to get it set up."

Dr. Grant Foreman was a local historian and author who was working to bring government jobs to the area. Having a past connection with the federal government, he knew people in Washington.

"That would be a perfect way for lots of people to see your work. I know you're a master at backdrops," she winked, "but have you ever painted a mural?"

"No, and it's entirely different than a typical painting or even a backdrop for a play. Blue Eagle has already starting giving us pointers on working at that scale."

"Oh, I hope this comes through. Wouldn't it be the perfect work for you?"

"Yeah, if you want government welfare work." Alex hid his frown behind his cup but Laura could hear the defeat in his voice.

"Oh, Alex, don't feel that way," Laura said, placing a hand over his on the table. "It's not your fault that the whole world is in a depression."

"I know," Alex shook his head. "But I can't keep letting you pay all the bills. It's not fair to you."

"Have I ever complained?"

"No," Alex blinked to hide tears. "Never. You've been so perfect, Laura. I don't deserve you." His voice took on a tone of irony. "That's the one thing your father and I agree on."

Laura was kept from replying by the arrival of Miss Wheeler to their table. The older attractive woman made a practice of making the rounds to greet patrons in her downtown restaurant.

"So how is the painting coming, Alex?" she asked after they had exchanged greetings. Miss Wheeler kept in touch with most of the art students in the renowned program at Bacone College.

"It's finally finished," Alex said. "I'm just waiting for Professor McIntosh's evaluation. I'm hoping for mercy."

"Oh, don't talk like that Alex," Laura chided. "You know you don't need mercy."

"No, Alex, don't," Nettie agreed. "Most of Blue Eagle's students have a painting or two on my walls. So I know what I'm talking about when I say you are his most talented student."

"You're too kind."

"Don't forget," Nettie reminded the young man. "I want you to enter it in the competition that Mr. Gilcrease is sponsoring. Paintings must be submitted by January 15."

Thomas Gilcrease, a Tulsa oilman, was a great patron and collector of American art, especially western and Native American art.

"Oh, Miss Wheeler, I don't know," Alex sighed. "I think I should just try to sell the painting."

"Nonsense," Nettie huffed. "This is a golden opportunity and I have no doubt you have a very good chance of winning. You bring that painting by to let me see it as soon as you can. We'll discuss the competition then and about getting it framed. You cannot submit it without a frame."

"Yes, Miss Wheeler," Alex said dutifully, giving Laura an amused look.

The self-proclaimed art critic patted his shoulder and then moved on to other patrons.

Laura imitated the woman's stern voice. "You bring that painting home for me to see, young man, before anyone else looks at it."

"Yes, ma'am," Alex laughed.

With the mood lightened now, the couple drained their cups, donned their coats and stepped outside to make the walk home to their tiny garage apartment. They had to pass the Rigsby mansion on their way, but neither said a word about the enormous stone house already decorated for Christmas.

As he always did when they were near Laura's childhood home, Alex kept up a story about something funny to distract her. He did not want to see the inevitable look of sadness that would cross his wife's face when reminded that she was no longer welcome in this palatial house. It killed him to see his wife sad. So he made her laugh and neither looked at the brightly lit greenery hanging in the entryway.

They were not aware that Mrs. Clara Rigsby just happened to descend the grand staircase to the foyer in time to see her daughter and son-in-law pass the front walkway. She paused to watch them. Their faces were animated in conversation and she thought they looked rather shabby . . . and very happy. She didn't know whether to smile or cry.

"What are you standing there for, dear?" Sam Rigsby asked as he too descended the stairs knowing their cook would have the noon meal ready to put on the table soon.

Clara turned quickly, blinking tears away. "Nothing, dear, I was just admiring the Christmas tree in the living room. It's a good one this year, don't you think?"

"I suppose," her husband replied. "I thought you were looking at something outside."

"No," Laura's mother said quickly. "Come; let's get to the dinner table. Cook will scold us if we let her salmon get cold."

Chapter 2

The following Monday, Alex sat in the art classroom with the other students waiting for the professor's evaluations on this semester's final assignment. He sat on a stool at his customary easel, trying not to appear as nervous as he felt. The large oil painting he had labored on for hours rested on the easel in front of him.

The smell of paint and mineral spirits gave the room its distinctive character. Alex knew he could find the room blindfolded just by following that wonderful, heady scent.

Professor McIntosh made his way around the room, handing his evaluations to each student. Occasionally he would offer a word of praise or constructive criticism; sometimes he would pat an arm sympathetically. McIntosh, known to the art world as Blue Eagle, was a brilliant artist himself, but he was rarely harsh in his criticism. He understood the slow process of channeling a student's raw talent into true craftsmanship and that each artist needed to be encouraged to move at their own pace.

Alex started swiveling back and forth on the stool. When he realized what he was doing he made himself stop. He was fidgeting like a kid in junior high. Joan, the student sitting at the next easel, gave him a sympathetic smile.

It was at times like this he wished he had not chosen an easel at the back of the room. It took a very long time for the teacher to reach him. Normally he liked the spot because of the natural light that streamed through the windows behind him. But waiting for a grade was nerve-wracking. So much was riding on this particular painting.

The professor finally reached him and handed him the evaluation form. Alex quickly glanced at the bottom of the page where the scoring was tallied. He had received a 96 out of 100. Relief flooded his soul. He had poured so much into this piece, telling a personal family story through brush strokes on canvas.

"A very good use of color, Barnett," the teacher complimented him. "I understand that you're planning to enter it into the Gilcrease competition. I think you'll do well."

"Thank you, sir." Alex wanted to ask more questions but the professor moved on to other students waiting for their grade. So the young painter glanced through the evaluation form. He read more encouraging remarks along with the scores for the various criteria.

The clock in the chapel steeple began to chime the half hour signaling that this class was complete. Since the teacher had told the students to be prepared to take their paintings home today, Alex reached for the large portfolio case he had brought. He pulled out a square of chamois cloth and tucked it around the painting then slipped it carefully into his case.

This was his last class for the day and the last for the semester as well. Alex walked to the campus trolley stop trying to keep a stiff wind from catching the large portfolio and pulling it out of his hands. Suddenly his painting felt more valuable than it had at any time while working on it this semester. The glow of kind praise from his teacher warmed him and gave him a sense of hope.

When the electric trolley pulled up to the stop, he joined other students in stepping aboard and dropping a token into the conductor's box. Then he took a seat near the back and set the portfolio down carefully, but kept hold of its handles. The faux leather case had been a gift from his late father a few years ago when Alex had declared his intentions of pursuing his art. It was showing its age now with scuffed edges and several scratches but Alex would have to make it do for at least a while longer.

The trolley clicked along the tracks carrying passengers from the school through the industrial area of town and into the central business district, making several stops along the way. Alex scanned the buildings they passed hoping to see a Help Wanted sign posted somewhere. But he saw nothing.

With classes out for winter break, he needed to find some type of work that would bring enough income to buy a gift for Laura. He had not forgotten about those perfect earrings at McEntee's.

When the car reached the Third Street stop, Alex joined most of the other riders in exiting into the downtown commercial district. Many hurried to do afternoon shopping or get to late shift jobs, but Alex took his time walking down Third Street. He did not stop at The Sugar Bowl though he was eager to show Miss Wheeler his painting. He had promised Laura that she would see it first, so he kept walking toward Calhoun's.

Alex paused to look into the bright storefront windows. He could see Laura standing at the perfume counter along the west wall of the store. She was helping a customer and he didn't want to interrupt a possible sale. Laura worked on commission and fortunately for them she was good at sales. She had a genuine interest in her customers and they trusted her to be honest about what fragrance would work best for them.

While Alex stood watching her work, a friend walked up and stood beside him. "See something pretty in there you'd like to have?" Charlie asked.

"I see something pretty I already have." Alex replied.

Charlie nodded in understanding. "You're a lucky man."

"I am a blessed man," Alex countered. "More than I deserve."

"Every man with a good wife can say that."

"Not every man knows it though."

"Very true," Charlie agreed. "You're rather philosophic today, college man. Is school out?"

"Today was the last day of classes and I'm glad. It's been a long semester for Laura and me."

"It's been a long year for everybody. You have a job lined up for your break?"

"No," Alex sighed, "and I need one. You don't know of anything, do you?"

"Not many jobs to be had. I'm grateful for the scraps Mr. Procter throws me."

George Procter was owner of all five movie theaters in downtown. Charlie worked as a runner carrying movie reels between the theaters. It didn't pay much, but it was a job. It gave Charlie, who was a musician, the chance to visit the theater in the thriving black business district that was jumping most evenings with jazz music.

Their small town was located half way between Dallas and Kansas City and was a usual stop for many musicians hopping trains to gigs in the larger cities. Muskogee would never have seen notable jazz greats had it not been for its location on the busy rail line. Charlie would sit in on jam sessions to supplement his income at the theaters and was becoming an accomplished jazz musician himself.

Charlie snapped his fingers as if he had just remembered something. "Say, I think Mr. Procter is hiring ushers for the Roxy. You might check with him about a job."

"Thanks, Charlie. I'll go to his office after I talk with Laura." Alex could see that her customer was carrying a small bag out of the store so he bid his friend goodbye and stepped inside.

Laura's face lit with pleasure when she saw her husband. Attempting a casual stroll across the store, he arrived at her counter with a smile of his own to match hers.

"Hey, girl," he greeted her and leaned down for a quick kiss. Laura looked around to make sure her supervisor wasn't watching.

"You know the rules," she said, matching his flirty tone. "No displays of affection while on the job."

Alex straightened up and assumed a formal posture. "Yes, ma'am," he said. Then he lifted the portfolio and set it carefully on the counter. "Could you tuck this back there for a while? I want to go see George Procter about a job."

"Is that your painting?" Laura asked eagerly, eyeing the case.

"Yes, but no peeking until I get back. I want to see your reaction to it."

"Well, then don't take very long. I don't know how much longer I can wait to see it. I've already waited all semester."

"I'll hurry if I can."

"What kind of job is Mr. Procter offering? Will he have you painting backdrops?" she smiled.

"I wish," Alex said ruefully. "No, it's a job as an usher. And I need to get to his office as soon as I can. Once the word gets out that he's hiring, there will be a line out the door."

Oh, alright, then go," she made a shooing motion with her hands. "I'll say a prayer."

"Thanks, babe." Alex looked around and gave her another quick kiss then turned and hurried to the door, pausing to hold it for several customers coming in to shop. He looked back at Laura and she held up crossed fingers.

Grinning, Alex left the shop then ran at a quick sprint around the corner to the Roxy. Mr. Procter had his offices on the second floor of the theater behind the balcony. He paused to catch his breath after taking the stairs two at a time. There wasn't yet a line of job applicants so he paused for several seconds to catch his breath and straighten his clothes. Too late, he wondered if he should have changed before applying for a job. But he couldn't worry about that now.

He pushed open the door and stepped onto plush carpeting in a rich burgundy. It matched the wallpaper and curtains in the theater itself. A receptionist sat at a desk of rich cherry wood. Even in the midst of a depression, Mr. Procter seemed to have suffered little economically. The movies provided an affordable diversion from the real world and the theater owner was happy to provide it for Muskogee and all the smaller towns around.

Alex knew from his reputation that Mr. Procter was a generous man. He freely gave away tickets to his movies, plays and vaudeville acts if he hadn't sold out by the time of opening curtain. Members of the all-boy marching band were regular recipients of his generosity and their band director repaid the favor by holding a free concert at the Roxy each Christmas.

Other kids not in the band knew to hang around the theater on Saturday mornings, hoping a few of those unsold movie tickets would come their way.

The receptionist, a young redhead, looked up from her typewriter when Alex entered the office. Her nameplate said she was Lillian Parker.

"May I help you?" she asked.

"Hello, I'm Alex Barnett. I was told Mr. Procter was hiring ushers. I wanted to apply."

Lillian looked him up and down, no doubt noticing his scuffed shoes and the frayed cuffs on his coat. He should have changed.

He remembered Laura's secret to the sale. He smiled, trying to make it seem genuine and friendly . . . not desperate.

"You'll have to fill out an application," was all Lillian said. She reached into a drawer for a sheet of paper, slid it onto a clipboard and handed the board and a pencil to Alex. "You can sit over there."

"Thank you." Alex took the clipboard and settled into a nice burgundy leather chair, remembering to sit up straight and not slouch. He wrote neatly, filling in the blank lines on the application.

When he came to "Current or Previous Occupation," he paused, wondering what to write. He had worked since he was in high school but mostly at odd jobs that lasted for a summer or other school break. He had cut grass and chopped firewood, washed windows and painted signs. Every penny had been saved for college, but that left no pennies for anything else.

He sighed as he stared at that blank line for a long moment. Looking back over his life depressed him. Maybe his father-in-law was right. Maybe he was a failure.

Alex had paused so long he became aware that Lillian was watching him. It shouldn't take this long to fill out a one-page application. Finally he took a deep breath and wrote, "Artist." It felt like a lie.

He slipped his smile back into place, stood and crossed the carpet to hand the clipboard to the receptionist. She briefly looked it over, then removed the paper and rose.

"I'll see if Mr. Procter wants to speak with you now."

"Thank you," Alex said, almost hoping the theater mogul would not have time. "If it's not convenient now, I can certainly come back at a better time."

"Have a seat," Lillian advised. "I'll only be a moment. I know Mr. Procter doesn't have any other appointments this afternoon and he's eager to hire extra ushers before Will Rogers' shows this weekend. I think he'll see you."

"So he's only hiring for the weekend?"

"Don't worry," the office worker smiled. "If you do a good job, he'll find a place for you. It might be only part-time at first though."

"That's fine. I'll take anything."

Lillian nodded, sympathy showing in her eyes. She must hear that sentiment often these days.

Alex returned to his chair and hurriedly tried to rub the scruffs from his shoes. He could hear the murmur of voices in the next office but could not tell what was being said. He added a prayer of his own to join Laura's.

Lillian crossed the even deeper pile carpet of Mr. Procter's office. Though he appreciated fine things, her boss was not a snob and Lillian certainly was grateful to have a job in such a nice office.

The man behind the large desk looked up when she entered. He was a small man, balding slightly and wearing glasses at the end of his nose.

"You have another usher applicant," Lillian said in answer to his unspoken question. She placed the application on his desk in front of him.

"That's the third one this afternoon," he mused, pulling off his glasses to rub his eyes. "How does word spread so quickly? I never even had to place an ad in the newspaper. Sam Rigsby won't be happy about that."

"You've given him enough business advertising the Will Rogers show; he shouldn't complain."

"There's no telling what Rigsby will complain about. It's his favorite pastime."

Procter put his glasses on and studied the application. "Who is this Alex Barnett? You know him? That name sounds familiar."

"I believe he's the young man who married Sam Rigsby's daughter Laura."

"You don't say. An artist?" he asked, noting the answer Alex had finally written on the occupation line.

"A student at Bacone." Lillian pointed to the "Education" line. "If I'm remembering correctly, he's a good artist, at least according to Miss Wheeler at The Sugar Bowl."

"Hmm," Procter studied the application thoughtfully. "Well, I can support young artists as well as Nettie Wheeler. Send him in."

"Yes, sir." Lillian crossed to the door, but before opening it she turned back. "Are you sure about this, Mr. Procter? I don't know how Mr. Rigsby might react to you hiring his son-in-law. The rumors around town say he doesn't care for him much."

Procter leaned back in his chair to ponder the matter. "He probably won't like it. I've heard Rigsby disparage the young man for no other reason than the fact that he is an artist. The man has no appreciation for the arts. Won't even come out to see a play unless Clara insists on it for the sake of appearances. If it doesn't boil down to dollars and cents Rigsby has little use for it."

"So I hear," Lillian demurely agreed with a smile. "And he probably doesn't care for vaudeville. He likely won't come to this weekend's show."

Her boss grinned. "You're right, though his newspaper carries Will's column. Send Barnett in. Then find him a uniform."

"Yes, sir."

When Lillian returned to the reception area, Alex stood, prepared to hear that he would need to come back later. He had removed his frayed coat and tried to smooth any wrinkles out of his Bacone sweater. He hated the way the red sweater clashed with the burgundy furnishings. Then he laughed at himself. Only an artist would notice or care about such things.

"Mr. Procter can see you. Go ahead and step back."

"Thank you," Alex said, trying to read from Lillian's smile whether she was trying to be encouraging or simply compassionate.

Alex entered the inner office and waited at the door, taking a moment to look around the generous space. The theater owner clearly appreciated art for several paintings and sculptures adorned the walls and bookshelves. He felt a little more encouraged.

Mr. Procter looked up from his reading and waved him toward the desk then stood to shake the young man's hand. "Have a seat."

Alex did so hoping his nerves didn't show. He had never interviewed for a job in such nice surroundings.

Mr. Procter held up the application and glanced over it again. "An artist, eh?"

Alex tried not to squirm in his chair. "Yes, sir."

"Know anything about ushering?"

"Only what I have observed from attending shows here," the young man answered honestly.

"In truth, there's not much to it, but you would be surprised how many young men don't get it. You have to care about people. That's really what it boils down to. Be courteous and helpful; try to anticipate the needs of our patrons."

Procter paused, looking at Alex over his glasses. "You think you can do that?"

"Yes, sir." Alex had always tried to give any job his best effort and this one would be no different.

After just a few more questions, Mr. Procter was asking if he could report for work the next day for training.

"Yes, sir," Alex agreed, gratitude swelling in his chest. "Thank you so much, sir."

"Do a good job at the follies this weekend and we'll see about something more permanent."

"I appreciate that so much, sir. I'll do my best."

Procter nodded and studied him for a moment. "See Miss Parker about your uniform. Keep it looking sharp."

"I will, sir," Alex promised, wondering if the remark was a veiled comment on his rather rumpled appearance. But he saw nothing mean-spirited in the man's eyes. He knew what disdain looked like. He had seen it often at the Rigsby home when he and Laura had been courting.

He felt such a weight off his shoulders as he stepped back into the front office. The pay was rather paltry, but he wouldn't complain. If he saved every single penny he earned before Christmas perhaps he would have enough to buy those earrings – Laura's earrings. He prayed no one else bought them before he could.

Miss Parker had already found a uniform and had placed in beside his coat. Black pants, a crisp white shirt and burgundy vest made up the ensemble. Alex was surprised that she had known he would be hired, but perhaps she knew her boss quite well.

"If it doesn't fit, let me know tomorrow and I'll find something else. There are white gloves and a black tie in the pockets. You'll wear those for the evening performances."

"Thank you. You must get good at guessing sizes. These look like they'll fit perfectly."

"You have no idea," Lillian smiled. "Ushering doesn't pay well so we have a regular turnover."

She helped Alex fold the clothing and put it into a large white box.

"When you arrive tomorrow see Mr. Sims in accounting at the end of the hall. He'll have some paperwork for you to complete so you can get paid."

"I will," Alex smiled. "Thank you again."

He took the stairs at a sedate pace that didn't match the racing of his heart. But he jumped the last two steps with a whoop that would make any Bacone Warrior proud. He had a job!

Instead of going to Second Street where Calhoun's stood, he walked briskly to Third Street to McEntee's with its clanging cuckoos. To his relief the earrings were still sitting in the window. He would need to inquire about the price to see if it was even remotely possible to purchase them, but today he just wanted to get back to Laura to tell her the good news.

Chapter 3

Laura was thrilled that her sweet husband had found a job. Since she had made several Christmas sales that afternoon, she insisted on buying some burgers at the White Owl Diner. They were running a special on their wonderfully greasy burgers – five cents each or six for a quarter and the hot, fat fries were free.

With two straws in a frosty mug of root beer, Alex and Laura felt like Muskogee royalty as they sat in a booth enjoying the meal. The tiny building sat right by the tracks and would shake whenever a trolley clanged by.

"So the job is only for the weekend?" Laura asked after they had eaten their fill of the diner's specialty burgers.

"Maybe," Alex said as he wiped his hands with the checked napkin. "But I think I'll be asked to stay on if I do a good job. Hopefully I can work around my class schedule next semester."

"Are you ok with ushering? I was so hoping it would be an art job."

"I'm happy with any job right now."

"Yes, I suppose we must be. At least it will be an indoor job through the winter. I worried about you last year when you were hauling and chopping wood."

"It built character," Alex smiled ruefully. "I've had a lot of character building in my life. Hopefully it's made me a good fellow."

"You're wonderful in my book." Laura leaned in toward him with a smile and their fingers intertwined on the table.

Alex glanced out the window at the glowing sunset. "We'd better get started home or we'll be walking in the dark."

"Yes, and I have waited long enough to see your painting."

The artist helped his wife with her coat and the two snuggled close as they walked briskly toward home with Alex carrying his still unopened portfolio and the box holding his uniform.

As they passed Second Street they could hear the sound of a jazz band playing at the Grand Theater, another of Mr. Procter's properties. Alex wondered if Charlie was sitting in with his saxophone.

They didn't linger at the downtown shops along Broadway where Christmas lights were strung across the street. Alex did notice that Laura paused just briefly at McEntee's where the silver earrings in the window reflected the festive lights.

When they reached the Rigsby home, cars were parked along the curb and the house had candles lit in every window.

"Must be the annual Christmas party for all the major advertisers at the newspaper," Laura noted. "Wonder who's parking cars this year?"

She turned to her husband with a conspiratorial smile. Last year it had been Alex and Charlie offering valet service to Mr. Rigsby's guests. Her smile took on a bittersweet look as she remembered that evening from a year ago.

It had been her mother's idea to get a couple of young men to help park cars for the holiday party last Christmas. There was only so much space along the curbs despite the fact that the Rigsby home and grounds took up nearly a whole city block.

The junior high school sat only two blocks away, however, so Clara received permission from the school to park cars there for the evening event. She asked Laura to help her find two young men who could move cars. Laura had known exactly who to ask.

Laura and Alex had been casual friends during their high school years. But the cute boy from the east side had really caught Laura's eye just before the Spring Dance their junior year. She was starring in the high school musical and Alex and the other students in shop class were building the sets for the play.

Mrs. Garrett, the drama and debate teacher, was not happy with the bland backdrop the shop students were installing and wondered aloud if she would have time to get an art student to paint something more interesting.

"Alex can do it," one of the boys volunteered his friend. "He's in art class and he can draw anything. Lickety split too."

All eyes turned to look at Alex, including the cast of the play. Laura had been unaware of the young man's talent until that moment.

"Can you, Alex?" Mrs. Garrett asked.

Alex looked at the plywood backdrop painted blue and green meant to represent sky and grass. It was ghastly as far as he was concerned and his fingers had been itching all morning to do something with it.

"Yes, ma'am," he said. "I believe I can."

"You believe you can or you know you can?" Mrs. Garrett challenged.

Doubts assailed the artist for a moment. He had never painted a scene on anything quite as large as a whole sheet of plywood before. "I, uh, I know I can," he finally stammered.

"Then get some paint and get to it. We only have three more days of rehearsal."

Alex grabbed Neal, the friend who had volunteered his talent, and the two boys hurried to the art room to explain the need for paints to Mrs. Brown. Soon they were back with the needed supplies and Alex was quickly absorbed in sketching out the details of the backdrop.

Rehearsal went on around him, but he barely heard the cast as they ran through their lines. Laura, however, could hardly concentrate on the play. She was fascinated with the beautiful scene flowing magically from Alex's quick, light brush strokes.

Looking back, Laura would mark this moment in time as the beginning of their relationship. And for her, their growing love was as beautiful as every painting Alex had ever done.

Her mother would have been appalled if she had known it was Laura who asked Alex to the Spring Dance a few days later. The popular young lady had figured out that this friendly, funny guy was no rebel who would dare to date one of the richest girls in school. So she had taken it upon herself to ask him in a casual, "Hey, you want to go with a group of us to the dance?" It was the first of many dates during their senior year.

Mr. Rigsby had never been enthusiastic about his daughter dating a young man from the wrong side of town but apparently had thought she would stop seeing him once they graduated. After all, they would never travel in the same social circles after high school.

At first they dated with a group of friends, often ending an evening at the movies or the skating rink with a stop at Laura's house for some sweet indulgence around the prep island in the big kitchen. Cook always kept fresh-baked chocolate chip cookies in a jar on the counter and the icebox was well-stocked with RC Cola and Grapette.

Mrs. Rigsby would occasionally come into the kitchen and visit with them all, making sure they had everything they needed. She smiled indulgently at Laura and her "little friends" and talked to them as if they were still in the sixth grade. Alex could tell that Laura was a bit embarrassed that her mother found it difficult to relate to teenagers. The newspaper mogul's wife was far more comfortable with her bridge club and service sorority.

One Saturday evening after a double feature at the Roxy, their group had arrived at the Rigsby home to find Cook had left out a Texas sheet cake, still warm from the oven. The three couples were gathered around the island, eyeing the cake with its thick layer of fudge frosting while Laura gathered plates and forks and a serving spatula.

"Alex, get the pop out of the icebox," she instructed and he went to do her bidding, pulling out the frosty bottles from the industrial-sized Coldspot.

Silence settled over the teens as they enjoyed the refreshments. After they had practically licked the cake crumbs off their plates, they set the dishes in the sink and then gathered around the big radio on the nearby counter, trying to pick up the broadcast from the Grand Ol' Opry.

Alex casually draped an arm across Laura's shoulder and they swayed to a static-filled Hank Williams tune. At that moment Mr. Rigsby came into the room having been informed by Cook that there was cake waiting in the kitchen and he'd better get some before those "hungry friends of Miss Laura eat it all."

Rigsby entered the kitchen and immediately stopped short at the door. His eyes fell on Alex just as all six of the friends turned to look at him. The man's eyes narrowed and sent a very clear, yet unspoken message. Alex lifted his arm off Laura's shoulder and took a half step away from her. Rigsby's stare made him feel as if he had been scorched.

Laura looked at Alex first then turned back to her father. She lifted her chin and met his gaze with one just as unflinching. Their battle of wills created tension in the room and Bert, one of the fellows, snapped off the radio mistakenly thinking Mr. Rigsby didn't like the noise.

The silence stretched on for what seemed a very long time but was actually only a few seconds. It was Mr. Rigsby who blinked. He took his gaze from Laura and Alex and looked instead at the half-eaten cake. Then he turned on his heel and left the room. But his message had been received by his daughter and her beau.

The next time their group was making plans for an evening out, Alex begged off, thinking to spare Laura her father's ire. But she would have none of that.

"My father doesn't get to decide who I go out with, Alex. I am already eighteen and an adult. I get to choose who I want to see and I want to keep seeing you. Don't you want that too?"

"You know I do, Laura. I'm crazy about you. But I don't want things to be bad between you and your parents. Not on account of me."

"They don't have to know."

"Laura, don't lie to them. I don't want you to have to do that."

"I won't lie; I just won't tell them anything about us unless they ask. And they won't ask. Mother is too busy and Daddy is rarely home."

Alex looked skeptical. He had been raised in church and taught that honesty and integrity were important character traits. "If your parents forbid you to see me, Laura, you have to respect that."

"They haven't forbidden me. Not in so many words. And if they do, I'll just move into my own place after graduation. I can get a job if I have to."

"Laura, I can't ask all of that of you."

"You haven't asked. It's my choice. What we do for love is not an obligation; it's a gift."

Alex smiled. It was the first declaration of love in their relationship and he was pleased that Laura had used the word for what had long resided in his own heart. "Then I will do whatever I need to do . . . for love."

From that point, Alex rarely came to the Rigsby house, but he and Laura spent time together nearly every day. After graduation, Laura did not move out, but she did take a job at Calhoun's Department Store. Mr. Rigsby wasn't thrilled that his daughter was working in such a public fashion, but Calhoun's was a major advertiser in his newspaper, so his protests didn't last long.

Not like his protests when he learned she was still seeing "that artist." It was almost exactly one year ago on the night of the annual Rigsby Christmas party. Laura had played the dutiful daughter for as long as she could stand, making small talk with the people her parents thought important enough to receive as invitation to their extravagant soiree.

Laura knew Alex and Charlie were outside shuttling cars on that cold night and she hated the thought of them trying to stay warm while waiting for the party to end.

She slipped into the kitchen where Cook was sliding petit fours onto two silver trays that the wait staff would carry to the guests. Decorated in glittery Christmas colors, the little cakes looked too pretty to eat.

Cook paused in her work to send a questioning look to the young heiress. "Miss Laura, what are you doing away from the party?"

"Mother, has moved it to the living room and Daddy is pouring drinks. You know she doesn't like me around alcohol. So I told her I would check on things in the kitchen."

Cook nodded and kept working, but wisely she left three of the petit fours off the big trays. Then she nodded to the two young women who had been hired for the evening and they carried the trays out of the kitchen.

"You want some hot cocoa for your friends outside?"

The older woman might be a servant with only an eighth grade education, but she was smart enough to see how things stood between Laura and that nice boy named Alex. It was no surprise to Cook that he was one of the valets outside.

"Thank you so much, Cook," Laura responded. "That would be wonderful." Laura came close and gave the sympathetic chef a peck on her cheek.

When the hot beverage was ready, Laura carried a small tray with the cocoa and cakes out to the back porch. The three friends huddled close around the tray enjoying the treat and laughing together.

When the first guests were ready to depart, a maid alerted the young men to get back on duty. They raced around to the front of the house to assist the departing party-goers.

Laura gathered up their dishes and walked into the kitchen to find her father had been standing at the back door. Apparently he had sent the maid out to alert the valets. There was a storm brewing on his face.

Laura stepped around him to set the dishes in the sink and place the serving tray back into a cabinet. She refused to meet her father's stare.

Finally he spoke. "What was that young man doing here?"

"Parking cars," Laura said. "Mother asked me to find someone to do that."

"I thought I made it clear that you were to have nothing more to do with him. Is he still courting you?"

Laura lifted her head to look her father in the eye. "No, I am courting him," she answered defiantly. "And he has a name. It's Alex Barnett."

"You are wasting your time with him. He has no future; he'll never amount to anything. The sooner you break it off with him the better." Her father's deep voice would carry well and Laura was quite sure their guests were hearing this exchange.

She lowered her voice to a whisper, hoping her father would do the same. "I don't plan to break up with Alex, Daddy. I believe he has a brilliant future as an artist and I want to be a part of it."

Her father must have understood her meaning for he looked shocked. "Can't you see that all he is interested in is your money? He is simply using you."

Laura wadded a napkin left on the counter and threw it into the sink of dishes. "Thank you, Daddy, for thinking so little of me. You must think I'm desperate or a very poor judge of character. I'm glad I know where I stand in your eyes."

"Laura, I never meant . . ." her father began.

But Laura turned on her heel and strode out of the kitchen, climbing the back stairs to the second floor. At first her anger left her cold and without emotion, but with time the tears came. She stood in the dark at her bedroom window watching the guests get into their cars as Alex and Charlie brought them around to the front walkway.

When it appeared most everyone had left, she quietly crept back downstairs and outside. She waited in the shadows while Cook handed the two young men each an envelope with their pay. They thanked her and then parted ways. Charlie headed north and Alex came around the back corner of the house to walk home.

"Alex," Laura whispered.

He paused and his eyes searched the shadows to find her.

"Laura, what are you doing out here? It's too cold."

"I wanted to see you." Laura tried to hide how upset she was, but Alex heard the tears in her voice.

He opened his arms and she walked into his embrace and cried softly against his shoulder. Slowly she shared the words she had exchanged with her father. They were words she had never since forgotten.

"I pity the poor fellows who are parking cars tonight," Alex quipped, breaking the reverie both had been in for a few moments and trying to lighten the mood. "They won't have a pretty girl sneaking cocoa and cake out to them."

"That was fun until Daddy caught me coming back inside."

"Don't think about that," Alex advised, pulling Laura a little closer. "I believe your father will come to regret his anger and his harsh words."

"Do you really think so?"

"I do. Your father isn't a bad man, Laura. He just doesn't value the same things we do."

Laura smiled. "You are a good fellow, Alex Barnett."

"Keep telling yourself that, my dear. Sometimes I feel like I'm not worth much of anything."

"You're worth the world to me," Laura whispered. The couple paused for a sweet kiss under the street lamp at the corner. Anyone in the Rigsby home looking out into the growing dusk would have seen them in that one soft pool of light.

Chapter 4

In a few minutes, they arrived at their apartment and hurried up the stairs. After they put away their coats, Laura pointed to the scuffed portfolio her husband had set on their tiny dining table tucked into the corner of the kitchen. "Ok, let me see it."

Alex waved toward the coffeepot. "Wouldn't you like some coffee first to warm up a bit?"

"No, I don't want coffee," Laura huffed. "Now hurry up."

Laughing, Alex slowly unzipped the case and carefully drew out the large painting. Pulling back the cloth he had wrapped it in, he set the painting against the wall and stepped back. He felt a bit nervous. Of all the people he wanted to please, Laura was the most important.

Laura took in a deep breath. "Oh, Alex, it's beautiful!" She rubbed her arms. "I'm getting goose bumps."

"I told you that you needed some coffee."

Laura punched Alex's arm. "That's not what I meant and you know it. This is so beautiful."

She leaned in closer to take in all the details of the exquisite painting. Done in what was coming to be called "the Bacone style," in clear bright colors the painting depicted an American Indian youth gazing into a sunset-tinged sky where a sliver of moon and a single star were suspended.

"It's the story of my great-grandfather," Alex explained. "His Osage name was Star-That-Travels. Do you remember?"

"Yes, it's such a beautiful story. He chose his name after hearing the Christmas message about the star that traveled and led the wise men to Bethlehem."

"That's right," Alex nodded. "I hoped to create something as beautiful as his story."

"You have, Alex," Laura assured him as she slipped her arm through his. "This is just amazing. It absolutely will win that art competition."

"I don't know," Alex said, pulling away a bit. "I think I should try to sell it. The cost of entering, not to mention getting a frame for it is more than I want to spend on something that's not a sure thing. We can't afford that right now."

"But you'll be making money at this new job."

Alex studied the painting, not wanting to meet Laura's gaze. He didn't want to tell her that he was determined to buy those heirloom earrings that perfectly matched her grandmother's locket. If what he earned as an usher wasn't enough, selling the painting was his only other option.

"Well, we'll see," was all he said. He could always create a new painting, but those earrings might only be available this Christmas. He so wanted to give them to Laura. After all that she had sacrificed for him, she deserved such a perfect gift.

Laura said nothing more, but she knew that stubborn set of her husband's jaw. Alex was able to endure a lot for the sake of his art, but she knew that he hated depending upon her paycheck for their living. She feared that if he found a buyer before the competition deadline, he would sell that exquisite painting. She was determined to keep that from happening and she thought she knew the way.

The following evening, George Procter stood at the edge of the balcony overlooking the auditorium below. The Roxy was full tonight and he was pleased. The band from Central High School was warming up on stage, preparing for their annual concert of Christmas music.

Glancing over the audience, he saw all the leading families in Muskogee were present as well as parents of band members. It was a good mix of people, the kind of audience Procter liked to see. It would do some of the stuffed shirts in this town a bit ofgood to mingle with folks from a different walk of life.

His thought made him smile, especially when he spotted Sam and Clara Rigsby entering the theater with Judge Martin. The magistrate had a nephew in the band and Procter knew from his wife that Clara Rigsby and Ellen Martin were good friends and bridge partners. Sam Rigsby looked bored but Clara chatted in a friendly manner with Ellen and the judge.

Seeing the Rigsbys made him remember to check on his newest usher, Alex Barnett. He spotted the young man at the front of the theater helping the elderly Mrs. Fred Watson into a seat. The woman was the matriarch of a ranching family and was nearly deaf. The ushers had a standing directive to help Mrs. Watson to the front. Everyone in the community knew very well to leave "Mrs. Watson's chair" empty.

Satisfied that everything was running smoothly, Procter walked downstairs to join the band director back stage. He would introduce the students, and then take his own reserved seat halfway back on the center aisle.

He checked his watch a couple of times then made sure the band director was in his place, baton at the ready. Procter knew he didn't need to see if all the band members were in their chairs. Mr. Getz never let a member of his band be late. If you were late, you were out of the band.

George parted the heavy burgundy curtains and stepped to a microphone at the center of the stage. He paused a moment for the lights to come down and the audience to grow quiet. He briefly looked around, noting all his ushers standing at attention along the walls waiting to show any last minute arrivals to the few remaining empty chairs.

"Ladies and gentlemen, the Roxy is pleased to present our annual Christmas concert with the Muskogee Central High School Marching Band. I give you the Pride of Muskogee!"

Applause erupted and Procter grasped the microphone stand and pulled it back inside the curtain. After he cleared the stage, the crew slowly raised the burgundy velvet with its gold fringe and the band began a jolly rendition of O Tannenbaum.

The theater owner quietly made his way to his seat and settled just in front of Judge Martin. The audience sang along with many of the familiar tunes and by intermission everyone was ready for a break to grab some popcorn or candy with coffee, or a slim glass bottle of pop. Outside the lobby, a food cart offered roasted pecans and spiced cider or hot cocoa.

Mr. Procter had slipped out just before intermission was announced to make sure all was ready in the concession booth. Once he was satisfied that the servers had everything under control there he prowled the restroom area and made a sweep of the balcony. The ushers were equally involved in canvassing the theater to be sure everything was in order.

Alex followed the head usher's lead and removed his gloves to pick up any trash that might have been dropped. While standing at his post along the outside wall, he had caught sight of Sam and Clara Rigsby sitting with their friends Judge Martin and his wife. Knowing they were in the theater made him a bit self-conscious. He could only hope that in the crush of people milling about they had not seen him.

Rigsby was studying the program, still looking bored while Clara and Ellen had stepped out to the restroom. Judge Martin had gone to get them all some popcorn and a soda. The newspaper publisher looked up just in time to see Alex reach for a program someone had dropped at the end of his row. The eyes of the two men met briefly, but they each pretended that they did not recognize the other.

For just a second Alex was glad that Laura wasn't speaking to her parents. He could only imagine what her father would have to say about his son-in-law working as a theater usher. It would hurt Laura and he never wanted that to happen again. It was bad enough that Rigsby had practically disowned her because she chose to marry a starving artist.

Alex moved on up the aisle, to deposit the program, a gum wrapper and a few pieces of dried popcorn into the trash receptacle in the lobby. He was pulling his gloves back on when Mrs. Rigsby walked by. Their eyes also met, but the reaction was different. Clara gave him a slight smile, then seemed to remember herself and looked away.

When she sat back down beside her husband, he wasted no time to remark. "Did you see who's working here?"

"Who, dear?" Clara kept her voice quiet and calm, as if hoping her husband could be persuaded to do the same.

"That Barnett kid."

"You mean our son-in-law?"

"You know who I mean." Rigsby pulled at his jacket lapels and sat a little taller as if asserting his superiority. "I knew he would come to something like this."

"Like this? Working at an honest job at a time when many men are begging for work?"

Rigsby's eyes narrowed. "Why do you always take his side?"

"I don't, dear. I'm just stating the facts of the situation."

"Well, this proves my point," he groused just loud enough for his wife to hear while waving his hand toward the young man being discussed as he helped folks return to their seats.

"What point?"

He gave an exasperated sigh. "That he was a good-for-nothing who would amount to nothing and was only marrying our daughter to get her money."

"Has he ever asked for any money?"

"Of course not, he knows what the answer would be. I made that very clear when they announced their engagement."

"Yes, and you humiliated our daughter in front of all our friends. It was not your finest moment, Sam."

"Well, she took me by surprise. I hadn't expected an engagement announcement. I just wanted her to understand the 'facts of the situation.' I wanted her to see this man for what he really was."

"Did it ever occur to you that your daughter is perfectly capable of judging character and that perhaps she was marrying Alex because she loved him and he loved her and your money had nothing to do with it?"

"I don't believe that for a moment. Just wait and see. Sooner or later he'll come around asking for help or he'll send Laura to beg for it."

"Really, Sam," Clara protested, still keeping her voice quiet as more and more people returned to their seats.

"Well, he won't get a dime of my money," Sam said, slapping his program against his knee to emphasize his point. "And I don't want you giving them any either. Do you understand?"

Clara waited a long moment to answer and only spoke when she realized the Martins had returned. "Yes, dear," she said, but the disapproval on her face said so much more.

Neither had paid any attention to the fact that George Procter had taken his seat in front of them and heard most of the conversation.

Chapter 5

The next day, all employees at the Roxy reported for work early to get the theater ready for their prestigious guest – humorist and favorite son Will Rogers with his follies repertoire. A front row of theater seats had to be removed to create an orchestra pit and several rolled up backdrops had to be moved from storage into place at the back of the stage.

The cleaning crew was polishing all the brass fixtures until they glistened. Even Charlie, who normally just ran the reels between theaters, was present and working with the stage crew.

Alex carried seats from the floor of the theater to create an additional row in the balcony. All three performances had already sold out. If there were no-shows for any of them Mr. Procter would hand out tickets to anyone available. He wanted a packed house for their prestigious guest who had actually been nominated for President two years earlier.

Suddenly there was a crash that reverberated throughout the building. Alex paused from bolting down a chair to look toward the stage. One of the backdrops had slipped from its track and fell in a crumpled heap. Alex could see the stricken face of his friend Charlie who had been working with some of the backstage crew to wrestle the large canvas into place.

Everything went silent as if the whole workforce was holding its breath in shock. Mr. Procter hurried from his office and rushed downstairs.

"What happened?" he asked sharply.

The stage hands were silent for a moment, none wanting to blame the others but none willing to take the blame themselves.

"Well?" Procter asked again as he approached the stage from the center aisle.

Finally the crew chief started down the ladder he had been standing on to help lift the backdrop into place. "Sorry, Mr. Procter. The canvas slipped and none of us could catch it. We all tried."

"Is is still usable."

"We were just about to check that."

The crew carefully lifted the canvas depicting a ranching scene with paid advertisements lining the sides. A large tear cut across the center of the backdrop.

Procter grabbed what hair he had. "It is far too late to get another backdrop made. Can it be repaired?"

Woody ran his hand along the ripped canvas. "We could tape it," he said, "and it should hold since the tear doesn't reach the edge."

Procter rushed up the steps to the stage. He approached the canvas that Charlie and Woody held up. "Tape will look cheap and tacky unless we can paint over it. I'll have to see if I can find an artist who can work on it this afternoon."

Charlie looked up to see Alex standing at the balcony rail. "You already have an artist, Mr. Procter."

The theater boss looked at him and then followed Charlie's nod toward the balcony.

"Yes," he said, thoughtfully. Then with growing excitement, "yes, we do."

Procter turned and cupped his hands to his mouth. "Barnett, get down here."

By the time he reached the stage, Alex's heart was pounding and not just from his run up and down stairs. He had not been able to hear all of the conversation on stage, but he suspected that Charlie had thrown him an opportunity to work on the painted backdrop.

When he stepped onto the stage, Procter immediately asked, "If I get you the paint, can you help us repair this tear?"

Alex studied the ranching scene. "Yes, sir. I believe I can."

"You believe? Or you know?" Procter might be glad to have an artist on his payroll, but he wanted to be sure the job would be done right.

Alex hesitated. It looked simple enough and he was sure that he could match the style of the original artist, if he could match the colors. Charlie gave him a nod of encouragement. "With the right paints, I know I can."

"Good. Woody show Barnett what we have backstage. If we don't have the paint he needs I'll send Lillian with a list to the Art Shop. Get the canvas taped as quickly and neatly as you can.

Barnett will need a smooth surface to work on. Won't you?"

"Yes, sir."

"Then get to it. If this doesn't work, we'll have to rush in a new blank canvas. We can't have the Cherokee Kid doing rope tricks in front of a Parisian bakery or an Italian canal. Everybody get busy!"

The crew sprang into action in a rush to do the boss's bidding. Alex picked out the paints he thought would work, and then found an old scrap of canvas to test the colors against the original. It had faded a bit so he knew he would need more white to soften the new colors. He sent Charlie with a list of the needed paints to give to Lillian.

In the meantime Woody had his crew lay the backdrop flat and then they removed their shoes and carefully walked to the center of the canvas and applied tape to the tear. Alex studied the scene on the canvas. It was larger than anything he had ever painted before, but fortunately only a small section needed work.

At his instruction, Charlie and Woody rolled the canvas around a long dowel and settled it between two ladders. The perspective would be off if he tried to paint it while lying flat. Soon he was absorbed in the work, only vaguely aware that the other workers would pause from their duties every now and again to watch him.

Occasionally George Proctor would step to the balcony rail and also watch the young artist. When Lillian walked by on her way to lunch she too stopped to admire Alex's work.

"Nettie Wheeler is right," she said. "He's going to be a great artist someday."

"I think he already is," her boss agreed.

"I'm going to the Sugar Bowl. Do you want me to bring something for you?"

"Yes, I don't want to take the time to step out today." He reached into his pocket and pulled out a money clip, peeling off a few bills. "Get whatever the sandwich of the day is. Chub doesn't make anything I don't like."

"Yes, sir." Lillian took the money and slipped it into her pocket then made her way downstairs. Procter continued to watch his artist, feeling as if he had just discovered gold.

"I wonder if he has a piece for sale," he thought out loud. "I'll have to find out."

At the Saturday evening follies, Alex helped patrons find their seats but kept an eye on "Mrs. Watson's chair." She had attended the Will Rogers performance the night before so he was sure she wouldn't need the seat today. If it remained unused, he planned to try to get a ticket for Laura who was working today at Calhoun's. She would be finishing her shift just as the performance was about to begin.

The theater filled quickly but that front seat remained open. He caught sight of Sam and Clara Rigsby and was surprised that the couple was attending the vaudeville show. But he supposed they had attended the dinner for the star held at the Severs Hotel today. Mr. Rigsby probably felt an obligation to come to the performance of his newspaper's most popular columnist.

When the lights first dimmed to alert everyone to take their seats, Alex stepped out to the ticket booth.

"Barbara, Mrs. Watson's seat is empty. Can I get a ticket for my wife?"

The young woman in the ticket booth sent an inquiring look to Mr. Procter who was greeting last minute arrivals and the boss gave her a nod.

She handed Alex a ticket but leaned close to whisper. "You can't leave your post. Mr. Procter won't stand for that."

"I know," Alex replied. "I have a plan."

"He worked his way through the lobby then hurried backstage where he knew Charlie was stationed to run for anything the performers might need. Alex had told Charlie his plan so he didn't have to explain when he handed him the ticket.

"You'll need to hurry to Calhoun's to catch Laura before she leaves."

"Does she know I'm coming?"

"No, I wanted it to be a surprise."

Charlie nodded then quickly donned his coat and stepped out the back door into the alley. The Roxy Theater shared the alley with Calhoun's so Charlie was already entering the large store by the time Alex returned to his post.

The runner spotted Laura reaching for her coat in the employee cloakroom.

"Hey, Laura," he said, coming up behind him.

"Charlie, what are you doing here? Aren't you working tonight?"

"Yes, Alex sent me." He pulled the Follies ticket from his pocket and with a dramatic flair presented it to her. "For you, madam."

Laura stared in surprise at the brightly printed ticket. "For me? There's a seat left?"

"Yes, but only if we hurry. Alex will try to save it for you."

"Then let's go."

They arrived backstage and Charlie led Laura through the labyrinth of lights, ropes and stage props. He opened a hall door for her. "Take this past the restrooms then go through the lobby to the main floor. The seat is down front."

"Oh, everyone will see me," Laura hesitated.

"Go! Alex really wanted to get you that ticket."

Laura smiled. "Thanks, Charlie."

The lights were already down by the time she reached the audience area. She strained to see Alex and finally caught sight of him waving her forward. He had just shown her the seat when Mr. Procter stepped out into the spotlight.

Alex moved to his post, his back resting against the wall. Having seen yesterday's show, he spent the evening watching Laura instead. He saw the pleasure on her face as she enjoyed the dances and songs and jokes.

He winked at her at intermission, but his duties kept him from conversation for a while. Then she stepped out into the aisle and approached him.

"I wonder if you could direct me to the ladies' room," she said with a mischievous smile.

"Why certainly, ma'am," Alex responded in the same tone. "Just follow me."

Alex had hoped they might find a quiet spot where they could exchange a few words but the whole theater was crowded. So he pointed her to the lounge area where dozens of women waited in line.

"Thank you," Laura said. Then she whispered, "This was the perfect Christmas gift."

"This wasn't a Christmas gift," Alex said, frowning just a little.

"But it should be," Laura countered. "You don't have to get me anything else."

"I'm not going to give you a gift that didn't cost me anything."

"But it cost you thought and time. And it's been wonderful."

Alex looked vexed. "I'm not so destitute that I can't get my wife a real present," he said in a quiet, controlled tone that said he was hurt and perhaps angry.

"I didn't mean that, Alex. Please don't be upset."

"I'm not," he lied. "I need to get back inside. Can you find your way back to your seat?"

"Yes." Her voice sounded forlorn.

Alex left her standing in the line to the restroom. She watched him weave through the crowd in the lobby hoping he would turn back with a smile to reassure her. But he didn't look her way.

Laura fought back tears, feeling miserable. She hadn't meant her remark to hurt him. She had been looking for a way to suggest they not exchange gifts this Christmas but her attempt had come out so badly. She could only pray that her words didn't push his pride to do something like selling his painting before the January competition.

She was fishing through her pocketbook for a handkerchief when she saw her mother step out of the ladies' room. She looked up to meet her mother's gaze and she quickly blinked back her tears and smiled.

Clara came and stood by her daughter. "It's so good to see you, dear," she said, longing in her voice.

"Yes, it is, Mother."

"Are you well?"

"I'm fine," Laura hastened to assure her. "I have a bit of a cold, I guess." She dabbed at her nose.

"Are you warm where you live?"

"Of course, Mother," Laura felt annoyance at the question. "We're as snug as two bugs."

"Good." Clara looked around to make sure her husband wasn't nearby. "You know you can come to visit me. Your father never said you weren't welcome."

"He made it clear that Alex wasn't welcome. I can think of no reason to come without him so I won't come until that changes."

Clara nodded then reached for Laura's hand and squeezed it. "I miss you."

Laura dabbed at her nose again. "I miss you too."

"Your father is a proud man, Laura, but I know he misses you as well. He loves you."

"He cares more about his money and his standing in the community than he cares about me or my feelings."

"He said things he didn't really mean and now he doesn't know how to take them back. You can understand that, can't you?"

Laura remembered her own words to Alex just a few minutes earlier. So yes, she understood saying something hurtful without meaning too. But her father's words had not been a mere slip of the tongue. He had spoken in anger and she would not soon forget it.

"I understand what he said, Mother. It was clear."

"Try to come visit me," her mother gently pleaded. "Come during the day when he's not at home."

Laura felt sorry for her mother, caught in the middle like she was. "I'll see," was all she would promise.

Clara nodded and then turned to go back to her seat. Laura stuffed her handkerchief back into her purse and then started down the aisle to her chair. She passed Alex, but he was helping a rather portly lady who was likely sweltering in her mink coat. They didn't speak.

For the second half of the performance the famous humorist had changed from his cowboy regalia into a business suit. He held a newspaper and spent another half hour providing commentary on the headlines. Rogers mostly poked fun at politicians and entertainers all while vigorously chewing a wad of gum.

"I'm not a real movie star," he told the crowd. "I've been married to the same women for twenty-eight years." Like all his other witty comments this met with appreciative laughter.

At the end of the performance, Rogers thanked the audience then stepped back to let the curtain fall. He was called back by the audience's standing ovation and requests for "more, more."

So the curtain rose again and he kept his commentary going while stepping out onto the piano in the orchestra pit. Then he stepped down to the piano bench and then the floor, talking all the while.

The cowboy humorist made his way up the center aisle shaking hands with patrons and delighting them with personal comments here and there. When he reached the back of the theater he raised his hand to wave and said, "Well, this old Okie needs to get back to California. You know when we Okies left Oklahoma to go to California we raised the IQ level of both states."

The audience roared their approval and then their hero disappeared through the swinging double doors and stepped out into the night where his driver was waiting.

Alex had kept his head down through the second-half monologue barely hearing the jokes and the laughter. He spent the time chiding himself for letting Laura's words bother him. In every way she tried to encourage him and support his art and he had no reason to feel hurt. But she was wrong if she thought he couldn't buy her a gift. Those earrings would be hers on Christmas morning, whatever it took.

For now, he knew he needed to make amends for his curt tone. So as the audience began to disperse he hurried to her chair before she could don her coat.

"Hey, wait here for a bit until I can get away. Then we'll get some roasted nuts and walk home. Ok?" He searched her face, hoping she wasn't angry at him.

"Ok," she agreed, but was careful not to say anything else.

Alex tried to keep his patience while the audience seemed in no hurry to leave. He couldn't clock out until the theater was clear. Thankfully the ushers wouldn't have to clean up because the theater would be closed tomorrow and the weekend cleaning crew would handle that detail.

Finally he was able to get his own coat and join Laura where she sat waiting for him.

"You ready?" he asked.

"Yes," she stood and stepped into the aisle. Alex took her hand and drew it around his arm.

"I'm sorry for being stupid earlier," he apologized.

"I'm sorry too. My words came out wrong."

"Let's forget it," Alex proposed. "How about we agree to just one Christmas gift for each of us?"

"Yes," Laura nodded. "Let's do that."

They walked by the McEntee's window on the way home and Alex casually checked to see that the silver jewelry still sat among the clocks as if waiting for him to purchase them.

Chapter 6

Alex noticed that Laura was wearing her grandmother's locket the next morning as they walked to church. The heart-shaped pendant was the "something old" Laura had worn for their wedding.

Her grandmother had given it to her to show her support for the young couple who were getting married without her parents being present. The antique piece had been one of Grandmother's own wedding gifts from many years ago.

Laura usually wore the silver piece with a lacy white blouse which suited the old-fashioned style of the pendant. Having looked at the earrings at McEntee's so often, Alex knew they matched the necklace perfectly.

They took their usual pew at church and the couple let the music of the organ settle around them and soothe their ruffled spirits. Alex found it inspiring to lift his eyes to the beautiful stained glass windows. Some of the ideas for his paintings came from studying these works of art.

After the pastor closed the morning service, the couple stood and began to mingle with others in the congregation. Laura's friend Cassie came to give her a hug.

"I haven't seen you in forever," she said when they separated.

"It's a busy time," Laura agreed. "I'm working a lot and Alex has started a new job too."

"Wonderful," her friend replied. "I see you're wearing that gorgeous necklace. You know my offer to buy it still stands. I have a customer who collects that type of jewelry and I know I could get a good price for it."

Cassie ran a little antiques shop on Main Street and this wasn't the first time she had offered to purchase the pendant.

"You know it's not for sale," Laura shook her head. "I couldn't part with Grandmother's locket."

"No, she couldn't," Alex agreed somewhat forcefully. "That's her connection to family, Cassie. We aren't so hard up that we need to sell our heirlooms."

"Don't get your dander up, Alex," Cassie chided without anger. "Times are hard for everyone. There's no shame in it. I didn't mean it as an insult."

Laura gave Alex a puzzled look. He had never seemed so protective of her necklace before. And it seemed odd that he was suddenly defensive about their finances. He had been told his job would continue at the Roxy. Why was he letting his pride show so much?

"I'm sorry, Cassie," Alex said. "I know you look at antiques like I look at paintings. I want to buy them all."

"That's exactly it," Cassie smiled. "Whenever I sell a piece that I've discovered and cleaned up it's like sending one of my children out into the world. I can only hope the buyer will love it and care for it as much as I do."

They all chuckled at her comment and Alex nodded in understanding. After investing part of yourself in a work of art, selling it was hard.

"Come by the shop sometime this week," Cassie invited Laura. "Bring your lunch and we'll catch up."

"I'll try," Laura promised. "Calhoun's is getting busy with Christmas so close."

"Well, then if I don't see you two before Christmas, I hope it's a merry one for you."

"Merry Christmas to you, Cassie," Laura agreed and the two friends hugged again before Cassie moved away to join her family.

Alex and Laura started toward the door but were stopped again; this time by Nettie Wheeler.

After exchanging greetings, Nettie wasted no time in asking, "Isn't school out? I've been waiting to see your painting."

"School is out," Alex said, "but I started a new job and haven't had much time."

"I'm glad to hear you're working, but I hope it won't take too much of your time away from your art."

"I don't think it will. I'm ushering at the Roxy and Mr. Procter says he may have me refresh all his backdrops."

"Well, how wonderful. George needs to update those dusty old things. Although I suppose he has less and less need of them. Movies seem to be replacing the music shows. But enough about George Procter. Can you come by the Sugar Bowl for lunch tomorrow, my treat?"

"We couldn't ask that of you, Miss Wheeler."
Laura demurred.

"Nonsense," Miss Wheeler tsked. "I'm not
above bribery if it will get you to bring that painting
in. I want to see it so we can decide what category
to enter it in for the art competition."

"About that, Miss Wheeler," Alex began, "I'm
not sure . . . "

"We'd love to come by tomorrow," Laura
interrupted her husband.

He looked at her in surprise. Laura was as
determined not to accept charity as he was so her
agreement to accept a free meal was out of character
for her.

"There's never a morning matinee on
Monday," his wife explained when she saw his
surprise. "You don't have to clock in until
afternoon, right?"

"Right," he agreed slowly.

"Miss Wheeler wants to see your painting,
Alex. She's waited all semester."

"Listen to your wife, young man. I'll expect
you around 11:00 so you can get Chub's fried
chicken. That's our Monday blue plate special and it
sells out fast. You don't want to be late and miss it."

"Yes, Miss Wheeler," Alex agreed. "I guess
we'll see you tomorrow morning and I'll bring the
painting"

"Wonderful. Have you had it framed yet?"

"No, I haven't," Alex hedged. He knew a
quality frame was expensive. He planned to only
have it framed if a potential buyer insisted on it.

"Good. I can help you with deciding on a style
and color, if you want my opinion that is." She
laughed at her words. "Excuse me for being so

pushy, but I know that the right frame can make a difference to art judges. It really does matter."

Laura and Alex exchanged a smile. Some folks said it was Miss Wheeler's "pushiness" that had kept her from ever marrying but Laura knew she had lost her fiancé in the Great War. Since then she had thrown herself into promoting young people and supporting others' dreams.

"Thank you, Miss Wheeler. I'm sure I can use your help," Alex told her.

"Then I'll see you tomorrow." The older woman's face was wreathed in smiles as she patted Alex's arm and then moved off to join a group of friends who always ate Sunday dinner together.

The couple walked home without much conversation. Both were absorbed in their own thoughts about a painting and a frame, a necklace and earrings and Christmas just two weeks away.

The next day, Laura left the apartment early, barely taking time to down coffee and toast for breakfast. Calhoun's was extending its shopping hours and would open earlier all this week. Hopefully that would give Laura enough sales opportunities to earn the money needed for a frame for Alex's painting.

She would not let him use the lack of a frame as a reason not to enter it into the art competition. If what Miss Wheeler said was true, this contest could give Alex the exposure he needed to find a buyer for this painting and collectors for many more to come. She would sell perfume like she never had before to have enough money to encourage his career.

The couple kissed goodbye, promising to meet at the Sugar Bowl for lunch. Alex stood at the front window and watched Laura carefully navigate around little patches of ice on the sidewalk. He would wait till he knew she was at work, then he too planned to walk downtown. He needed to pick up his first week's paycheck, cash it and then visit McEntee's to inquire about the earrings.

Alex knew this one paycheck likely wouldn't give him enough funds to purchase the jewelry, but perhaps he could persuade Jess McEntee to put them back for him until he got his next paycheck a week before Christmas. He had calculated over and over what his part-time hours would garner him and knew it would likely take every penny or more to buy Laura this gift.

At the theater, Alex left his portfolio in the backstage locker room and joined the other ushers standing in line outside Mr. Sims' office. He felt nervous as he waited for that precious piece of paper that would validate his worth as a wage earner. A job had never seemed as important to him as it did right now.

Alex knew he should act casual about receiving a paycheck, but he couldn't help tearing it open as he stepped out of line. He looked at the amount printed on the check above Mr. Procter's signature. It was less than what he had expected so he studied the paystub. There was a withholding for his uniform . . . something he had not anticipated.

His heart had fallen to the pit of his stomach as he slowly made his way downstairs. He would cash the check at the bank across from McEntee's and then . . . then he would pray he could buy those earrings without having to sell his painting.

He carefully pulled the portfolio holding that painting out of his locker and walked toward the lobby. Mr. Procter was just entering as he reached the exit.

"Good day, young man," Procter greeted him.

"Hello, Mr. Procter."

"What have you there, Barnett?"

Alex looked at the case and then remembered that his boss had an appreciation for art.

"It's a painting, sir. I was going to show it to Miss Wheeler at the Sugar Bowl."

"Can I see it?" Procter asked.

"Yes, sir." Alex set the case on a velvet-clad bench in the lobby and gently removed the wrapped canvas. He pulled back the chamois cloth and heard the other man gasp. But when he looked up at Mr. Procter the man's face was impassive. Was he impressed or appalled? Not everyone liked the Bacone style of Indian art.

Procter studied it for a long moment, eyes narrowed. "That's a fine piece, son," he said. "Is it for sale?"

"Well, Miss Wheeler wants me to enter it into an art competition in Tulsa. But I think I just need to sell it."

Procter stepped around Alex to look at the art piece from another angle. He nodded. "Nettie's right. That should go into an art show. But I want you to promise me something, all right?"

"Sir?"

"Promise me that after it wins and has toured the country, you'll give me first dibs on buying it. I ought to snap it up right now because I suspect you don't know how good it really is. But I won't do that. Nettie would have my hide. Just promise me that you'll give me a first bidder's discount because when the art world sees your work I won't be able to afford an Alex Barnett painting."

Alex was sure the theater owner was joking but his tone and his face said he was serious.

"Mr. Procter, I'll sell it to you right now."

"No, Nettie is right. You have to enter it into that competition. Then you come and see me about a sale."

The hope Alex had felt seemed to seep out of him like air out of a balloon. He was too proud to tell his boss that he couldn't afford to enter it into the Gilcrease competition. He couldn't afford the frame because he was going to buy earrings for his wife. So he said nothing, only nodding as he slipped the painting back into its case.

Procter patted his arm, gave him a smile and then walked on toward his office. Alex left the theater and walked slowly toward the bank. Who was he kidding? Apparently his painting was too good to sell and he couldn't afford to do anything else with it.

After cashing his check, he carefully folded the small sum and tucked it into his pocket. Then he crossed the street to the jeweler's. The clerk lifted the black velvet-line box out of the storefront window and let Alex look at the earrings more closely. They were flawless and obviously genuine silver.

"What is the price?" he asked, then steeled himself for the answer.

"Fifty dollars."

Alex felt his mouth drop open. If he worked until spring he wouldn't have enough to buy those earrings, not after paying college tuition and buying the art supplies he would need for classes next semester.

"I don't have the cash with me, right now," he said. "Could you put them back for me?"

The clerk looked him up and down. Alex knew he didn't look like someone who could afford such expensive earrings.

"I suppose," the man sniffed. "But only for a few days. We can't miss a sale while waiting on you."

"I understand," Alex nodded. "Just hold them a few days, ok?"

"Very well." The clerk set the box under the counter. Alex took up his portfolio and then walked toward the Sugar Bowl. The painting felt like lead.

Chapter 7

Alex sat at a table and sipped coffee for a few minutes, his mind whirling with ideas for how to satisfy everyone pulling at his life. Miss Wheeler and Mr. Procter seemed to be conspirators in keeping him from selling his painting. His worry over it was making him irritable and he had snapped more than once at his sweet wife in the past few days.

He should just forget the earrings but he couldn't do it. Laura had given so much for him. He was going to find a way to show her how much he loved her and how grateful he was to have her as his wife.

"Wow, you're deep in thought." Laura's voice broke through his musings.

"Oh, sorry," Alex said, standing to help her with her coat. "I was thinking pretty hard."

"If you've solved this Depression problem, you might give the President a call." Laura teased.

"Don't I wish." Alex tried to match her light tone.

"Has Miss Wheeler seen your painting?"

"Not yet. She's in the kitchen. Guess she's getting the staff all lined out for the lunch crowd."

It was just a few minutes later that Nettie stepped out of the kitchen and caught sight of the young couple. She spoke a moment to Susie the waitress then came to where they sat. Alex stood again and pulled out a chair for her.

"I can't sit," Nettie said. "We'll be busy in just a few minutes. You know what I want to see."

Alex smiled. "Yes, ma'am." He went through the same process of opening his case and carefully displaying the canvas.

Nettie said nothing at first. She put on her glasses that dangled from a chain around her neck. She leaned closer to the painting her eyes scanning it up and down.

Alex and Laura exchanged a bemused look while they waited. Finally the woman straightened and smiled. "This outshines anything I have ever hung on my walls," she said, her voice hushed. "You are fortunate, Alex, that Mr. Gilcrease is a patron of western art and has a category for this style. I have the entry form in my office and will be happy to help you fill it out. What are you calling this piece?"

"Star That Travels," Alex said. "But about that, Miss Wheeler . . ."

Just then Susie arrived with two blue plate specials – golden fried chicken, mashed potatoes with cream gravy, green beans and buttery yeast rolls.

Nettie lifted the painting away from the table so as not to risk getting food on it. Just then a regular patron entered the café. An older man with a shock of white hair immediately caught sight of

Nettie holding the painting. He made his way toward the table.

"What have you discovered, Nettie?" he asked while peeking over her shoulder at the canvas.

"Never you mind, Grant," Nettie said, handing the painting back to its creator. "Just find a seat and don't try to poach my protégé."

Grant Foreman held up his hands in mock surrender while winking at Alex. "If that's for sale, come see me," he said in a staged whisper.

Nettie shooed her fellow art patron away. "Get," she said. "It's not for sale right now."

Alex started to protest but shut his mouth without a word. Both Nettie and Laura had such determined looks on their faces, he knew he was outnumbered. If he sold this painting, he would have to do it secretly . . . and soon.

He covered the piece again and slid it back into the case. He knew where Dr. Foreman lived just a block from Laura's parents. Maybe he had found his answer.

After they finished sharing a slice of lemon meringue pie, Alex and Laura stood to leave. He glanced at his watch. "I need to get to the Roxy. My shift starts in just a few minutes." He reached down for the portfolio.

"Where are you going to keep your painting?" Laura asked.

"In the usher's locker room, I suppose."

Laura grimaced. "That doesn't sound very safe. Why don't you let me keep it at the store?"

Alex studied the case. "I suppose that would be better."

Laura held out her hand for it and as Alex hesitated, she smiled. "I'll take good care of it. I promise."

He relaxed and grinned. "I know you will." He handed the portfolio to her. "Now I need to go." He gave her a quick kiss.

"Don't forget I'm working late tonight," Laura reminded him.

"They're asking you to work late?"

"They didn't ask; I volunteered," Laura explained. "You're working late so I might as well. Besides a few extra dollars won't hurt at Christmas." She gave him a secretive smile.

"Don't spend it on me," he said. "I don't need anything special."

"Don't worry about it," was all Laura would say.

Alex shook his head and then hurried to the door. Laura followed at a slower pace. She stopped near the cash register and waited to catch Miss Wheeler's eye. When the café owner came to see what she needed, Laura asked, "Where can I get a frame?"

"Take it to the Art Shop," Nettie advised. "Tom's a friend of mine and will do a good job. I've already told him to expect Alex to come in. He'll know exactly what frame that piece needs."

"Thank you, Miss Wheeler." Laura started to leave but turned back. "Don't mention the frame to Alex, please. It's going to be my Christmas gift to him."

"I won't say a word," Nettie smiled. "And don't tell Alex that I am paying the entry fee for the competition."

"Oh, Miss Wheeler, we can't ask you to do that," Laura protested.

"You didn't ask. I volunteered," Nettie stated. "But we can call it a loan, if you prefer. You can pay me back out of the Grand Prize Alex is going to win."

"You really do believe he can win?"

"Well, I can't know what paintings will be entered into his category, but I know many of the artists working in that style. Alex is the best that I have seen."

Laura drew in a deep breath that carried hope and a prayer in it. "Thank you, Miss Wheeler, for everything."

"You're quite welcome."

Laura turned and left the café, making it back to her station at Calhoun's just in time to avoid a scolding from her supervisor. She would take the painting to the Art Shop on her supper break. Hopefully she could buy the frame and have the framer keep it until just before Christmas.

While Alex had showered this morning, she had pulled out all the money she could from the chipped cookie jar they kept at the back of a kitchen cabinet. It wasn't as much as she hoped for but she didn't dare take out the rent money which was due in just a few days.

Laura had no idea how much a frame for such a large painting would cost. She could only pray that she would have enough.

"How much?" Laura asked in disbelief a few hours later. Tom repeated the price, almost apologetically. The amount was twice as much as she had brought with her – twice as much as she possessed.

They had spent nearly the entire half hour looking at frames. Tom had quickly rejected the ornate gold ones and the carved cherry and oak ones. He had suggested a simpler frame of a grayed wood that made Laura think of old driftwood. It was a substantial size but its simplicity matched the style of the painting and perfectly complimented the star-silvered colors of the night scene. She had not expected that such a simple frame, even of that size, could cost so much.

"That cost includes the backing, hangers and assembly," Tom explained.

"Of course," Laura said, trying not to sound as shocked as she felt. Money had never been an object when she was growing up and she had rarely concerned herself with how much things cost. Since her marriage she had been forced to learn the hard reality of living on a limited budget and doing without.

"I wonder if I could pay something down today and come back a little closer to Christmas to get it. I don't have a place to keep it out of sight at home." She hoped her request didn't reveal the fact that she could not pay for the frame today.

"Sure, I'd be happy to," Tom said, "especially for a painting of that quality. Nettie told me your husband was talented but I had no idea he was that good. It will be an honor to have one of my frames embrace that painting."

Laura thought his description to be quite romantic and she felt tears threaten to spill. "Thank you so much. I'll be back late next week."

"The frame will be waiting for you," the shop owner assured her.

Laura walked back to the store and carefully set the portfolio behind the perfume counter. All evening she racked her brain for ideas for earning additional money. To make matters worse, there were few shoppers in the store and she only made one sale.

She had to acknowledge that she couldn't count on earning enough commissions to pay for the frame before Christmas. And she knew from what other clerks had told her that sales in January were usually low. They had advised her to save as much of her December earnings as possible to tide her through a slow month.

Laura thought about all the pretty things she had left at her parents' home. She had chosen to take none of her jewelry and had left all the party clothes and dozens of shoes behind in a massive closet. Not until today did she wish she had some of those items. Not until today had she felt such a desperate need for funds.

Laura remembered the locket her grandmother had given her on her wedding day. She would hate to sell it and she knew Alex wouldn't want her to give it up for him. No, selling the locket would have to be a last resort.

By closing time, Laura had decided to call on her mother during her lunch break the next day. She would not ask for money, but perhaps she could ask for some of her jewelry. Alex wouldn't have to know that she had done the one thing they had agreed never to do . . . ask her parents for help. She couldn't let prideful promises keep her from giving Alex this most important gift.

Chapter 8

The walk from Calhoun's to the Rigsby home might have been pleasant the following day had Laura not been filled with nervous guilt. The sun was shining and the air had warmed nicely by the time of her midday break, but she hardly noticed.

It felt odd to walk up to the front door and ring the bell to her old home. It took all her willpower not to turn and leave rather than wait for the maid to answer.

The massive oak door swung open silently. Laura saw surprise register on the maid's face.

"Hello, Josie," she greeted the young woman.

"Why, Miss Laura," Josie said. "What a surprise to see you."

"Is my mother home?"

"Yes, miss . . . I mean, ma'am. She's in her study . . . on the phone I think. Would you like to wait in the living room while I get her?"

"Yes. Thank you, Josie."

Josie swung the door open wider and Laura stepped inside.

"May I take your coat?"

"No, thank you. I can't stay long," Laura demurred.

Very well. I'll let your mother know you're here."

Josie disappeared down a hall beside the grand staircase. Laura unbuttoned her coat and stepped into the living room where a 12-foot Christmas tree dominated one corner. A fire snapped in the fireplace and the mantle displayed her mother's nutcracker collection. The room brought back a flood of mostly good memories and the young woman was swamped with unexpected homesickness.

She sank onto the ivory damask sofa and looked around at all the familiar furnishings and decorations in her mother's tasteful style. Nothing seemed to have changed yet she felt very out of place here. Laura supposed it was she who had changed.

She was studying the art deco ornaments on the tree when she heard her mother's footfall at the pocket doors of the living room. She turned to face the older woman, almost expecting a look of disapproval.

Instead Clara Rigsby opened her arms to offer a welcoming hug. Laura stood and went to her mother and they shared an embrace.

When they parted Clara had to dash away a tear. "I'm so glad you came, Laura. Let's sit. Or can you stay for lunch? I'll have Cook prepare something special."

"No, Mother, I can't stay long." Laura felt her nervousness return. Was she betraying Alex's trust by being here? She had vowed never to come home unless her husband was welcomed as well.

Her mother noted Laura's worried expression. "Is something wrong, dear? Have you left him?"

"What?" Laura now felt shock run through her. "Of course not! We're quite happy. Is that what you hoped?"

"I didn't say that, Laura. I just wondered why you had changed your mind about coming to visit."

"You invited me. And it's Christmas." Laura could not bring herself to reveal the real reason she had come. In that moment she knew she could not ask her parents for help.

"How much were you hoping to get from us?"

The deep timbre of her father's voice set off an earthquake of emotion in the room. Laura and her mother looked up to see Sam Rigsby standing in the doorway. Each had the same expression of shock on their faces. They had not heard his approach from the back of the house.

Her father's cynical tone felt like a bucket of cold water pouring over the younger woman. Laura straightened her backbone and braced for whatever unkind remarks he was sure to make.

"Sam!" Clara said, rising suddenly and going to her husband. "I wasn't expecting you home. Look who's come to visit. Isn't it wonderful?"

Rigsby looked from his wife to his daughter. "I would like to think it is. But you didn't come just for a visit, did you?"

Laura felt a flash of anger, even though his words hit at the truth. "What makes you think I'm here for money?" she dared ask.

"I told you he wouldn't be able to support you," her father answered. "I said it would be only a matter of time before you would regret your decision and would be back here with your hand out."

"Everyone is struggling to make ends meet right now, Daddy."

"I'm not. And you wouldn't be either if you had listened to me. An artist, indeed; theater usher is more like it."

"Alex is getting offers for his art. Just the other day Dr. Foreman said he'd buy his latest work."

"His wife will put a stop to that. Carolyn's the practical one of those two. Don't count on seeing a single penny for his art. Anyone in town who wants to do business with me will not do business with your husband."

"How dare you, Father," Laura replied, her voice low and laden with pain. "You sit here in your palace, judging me and my husband. You won't even say his name. You belittle him for his supposed lack of success yet you stand in the way of that success."

Laura stood to leave. "Don't worry, Daddy. I'm not here to take your money. I wouldn't take a penny from you even if you wrapped it in a bright red bow."

She pushed past her parents and hurried to the front door wanting to leave before the tears began to fall. She yanked the front door open and stumbled down the front stairs to the sidewalk, then turned to hurry home. She couldn't go back to work in such a state.

Her mother followed Laura to the door and stood watching as her only child hurried away. Then she turned to glare at her husband.

"How dare you send her running away again, Sam. We may have just lost her forever." Then she hurried up the stairs. Sam heard the door of her bedroom slam shut.

He stood in the silence of the foyer. The imperial look on his face slowly turned to one of regret. With a sigh, he also walked to the front door, stepped outside and closed it quietly. Then, looking defeated, the publisher trudged slowly back to the newspaper office.

Laura practically ran up the stairs to the apartment and fumbled with her key to open the door. She tossed her handbag on the kitchen table as she passed it and went into the bedroom. Yanking open a drawer in the bureau, she reached for a fresh handkerchief. The one from her purse had grown soggy from her tears.

Laura's eyes fell on the little locked jewelry case sitting on the bureau. She only kept it locked because of her grandmother's locket; nothing else inside was valuable. She stared at the case for a long moment, the hurt and anger still battling in her heart.

Finally, she opened another drawer and withdrew a key. Slowly she unlocked the jewelry box and lifted out the heart-shaped locket. She opened it to reveal a photo of Alex on one side and another photo of them together taken on their wedding day.

"I'm sorry, Grandmother," she whispered, "but I know you'll understand." Her grandmother was not a wealthy woman so a gift of such value had been a testament of her love for Laura.

The granddaughter sadly drew out the photos and slipped them into the jewelry box and locked it again. Then she took another handkerchief from the drawer and carefully wrapped the locket inside. She slipped the necklace into her coat pocket and then checked her appearance in the mirror.

She saw a determined face in the glass. "I won't let anything stand in Alex's way," Laura promised herself with resolve. She glanced over at the portfolio sitting in a corner of the bedroom. "Love is worth this sacrifice."

She was still telling herself that as she walked to Cassie's antiques shop after her shift ended that day. Cassie expressed surprise when Laura spread the handkerchief holding the necklace out on the little counter near the antique cash register.

"Do you still want to buy it?" Laura asked.

"Well, yes, but are you sure you want to sell it? You know I was teasing a little when I offered to buy it. I don't want you to feel any pressure from me."

"I don't," Laura assured her. "I'm glad I have a friend I can sell it to. I know you're honest and fair. I want to get a certain gift for Alex for Christmas."

Cassie still looked hesitant but she took up the necklace and studied it carefully. "This really is exquisite," she said then named a price that was just a few dollars less than the cost of the frame. With what she had saved out of their cookie jar bank, Laura would have enough for what she hoped would launch her husband's art career.

"I can't offer more than that," Cassie said apologetically. "I have to leave a little profit margin for myself."

"Don't apologize," Laura responded. "That's more than fair."

"Well, if you're sure . . ."

Laura took in a deep breath and nodded. "I'm sure."

Cassie opened the cash register and counted out the dollars into Laura's hand. Her friend folded the bills, tucked them into her pocketbook and turned to leave the little shop. Laura took the long way home to give herself enough time to cry and be over it by the time she reached the apartment. She didn't want Alex to suspect what had just transpired.

When she stepped in the door, she was shocked to see a large cedar Christmas tree standing at a lopsided angle in their living room. Alex was on his knees beside the tree, trying to get it to sit straight in a bucket of water and rocks.

"Where did you get that?" Laura asked, her surprise evident. The tree took up one corner of the room and was much larger than what they really needed. Laura had never planned for them to even have a Christmas tree. How did her husband find the money for such an extravagance?

Alex rocked back on his heels and studied the tree. "A farmer was setting up a lot across the street from the Roxy," he explained. "Charlie and I went over on our break and helped him unload the trees from his truck. So he offered us trees as his thanks. Charlie didn't want one so he told the man to give me a big one."

"Well, he certainly did that." Laura removed her coat and dropped it with her purse on the sofa. Then she stepped closer to take a sniff of the fragrant tree.

Alex's laughed. "Don't be too impressed," he advised. "This thing is so prickly he would have had a hard time selling it for much. I'm sure that's why he chose this one. You should have seen Charlie and me lugging it home."

Laura laughed at the image.

Alex stood and stepped back to check the tree's angle. Satisfied that it was now standing straight, he nodded. "There. It's ready to decorate."

"With what?" Laura asked, still laughing. "We don't have any decorations."

"We have popcorn," Alex waved a hand toward a half dozen tubs of theater popcorn tucked beside the sofa. "Plenty of popcorn. And if that's not enough, I know where I can get more."

The two of them laughed and money troubles were momentarily forgotten.

Chapter 9

A few days later, Alex stood in the kitchen staring at the Purity Drugstore calendar. Christmas was only one week away.

He had received his second paycheck the day before. While it was larger than his first check, it still wasn't enough to buy the earrings. "You know what you have to do," he told himself, keeping his voice low. "Buck up and do it."

Shortly Laura entered the kitchen wearing her lacy white blouse, but not her grandmother's locket. She poured herself a cup of coffee and then dropped a slice of bread in the toaster. She grimaced a little as she sipped the hot coffee. She used to drink it with lots of cream and sugar, but after her marriage she drank it black. It was far less expensive that way.

Alex studied her, thinking his wife seemed a little sad. "Don't you usually wear your grandmother's locket with that blouse?" he asked.

Laura automatically reached for the place where the heart-shaped pendant normally fell from its sterling chain. She felt a little flattered that Alex would notice such a detail, but at the same time didn't want him to pursue the matter.

"Oh, I was in a hurry, I guess," she said, not looking directly at him. "The clasp was sticking a little."

Turning away, she grabbed the toast as it popped up, then reached into the icebox for some apple butter. Smearing a thin layer on the bread, she still avoided her husband's eyes.

"What are your plans for today?" she asked. It was Alex's day off from the theater.

"Nothing much," he responded. "I can take some laundry downstairs." Their landlady let them use her wringer washer that she kept in the garage below them.

"Good," Laura said brightly. "We need some laundry done."

"Yeah," Alex agreed, feeling puzzled. Their conversation seemed stilted and he wasn't sure why. Did Laura suspect what he was really planning to do today?

Finishing her toast, Laura rinsed out her cup and washed the butter knife. She set them on a towel by the sink and then went to the closet for her coat.

Coming back into the kitchen while she buttoned it, she finally smiled at him. She took a brown paper sack holding a sandwich and apple out of the icebox. Then she kissed him goodbye and whispered, "Love you."

Alex impulsively pulled her closer for a longer kiss. She seemed surprised at his sudden fervor. But all he said was, "Love you too. Have a good day."

The kitchen clock ticked a few seconds while they met each other's gaze. Their eyes were filled with silent messages of love and commitment . . . and apologies for necessary sacrifices.

Laura looked at the clock and realized she needed to go. "I'll see you this evening," she said in a husky voice, then let herself out the door.

Alex sighed, then poured himself the last of the coffee. He would skip anything else for breakfast as he had for the last few weeks. Not that such measures had truly saved them much money, but he had felt the need to try. Good thing there was always plenty of left-over popcorn at the theater.

He downed the last of the coffee and rinsed out his cup to sit beside Laura's. He strode to the bedroom and grabbed the handles of his art case. He unzipped it to check that the protective cloth was still in place around the painting. It had slipped at one corner so he took a moment to tug it back into place.

His hands stilled and he drew a deep breath. He hadn't expected it to be this hard to sell the painting. After all that had been the goal all along while working on it during the past semester. He had spent hours on it, not just during the class period but often after classes were out for the day.

He studied the scene he had painted. The story passed down through family about his great-grandfather had made for a dramatic piece of art.

In a native tradition, his ancestor had spent the night alone on the prairie as a rite of passage into adulthood. The star – the guiding star of the Magi – had symbolically provided him guidance as well.

Alex had tried very hard to capture the wonder of it, the miracle of it. From everyone's reaction to the painting, he felt sure he had succeeded.

Alex really wanted to enter this very personal painting in the art contest Miss Wheeler had found for him. A win could be huge for his career. But those earrings wouldn't be available next Christmas. He had stopped at the jeweler's after cashing his check yesterday. The clerk told him he would only hold the earrings one more day because he knew someone else had an interest in them.

There would be time to paint something else for some future competition, perhaps something even better than this one. There was only this Christmas to get such a perfect gift for Laura and he knew the opportunity might never come again.

"Sorry, Miss Wheeler," he said as he closed the case. "I hope you'll understand. Some things are just more important. Laura has sacrificed so much for me . . . this is the least I can do for her."

Someday I'll do more, he promised himself as he pulled on his coat. Someday I will buy my wife cream and sugar so she doesn't have to drink her coffee black. Then he took up his portfolio and slipped out the door.

It took Alex only a short time to walk the few blocks to the Foreman house. The unpretentious old Victorian sat on the corner within sight of the Rigsby mansion. He stepped through the gate and went up the walk to the door. He had made an appointment with Dr. Foreman yesterday so he knew the noted author would be home.

He rapped on the front door using an ornate knocker. Shortly the houseman came and opened it.

"Hello, Pressley," Alex greeted him. "I have an appointment with Dr. Foreman."

"Yes, sir," the man stated as if had been expecting Alex. "Dr. Foreman is out back putting seed in the bird feeders. You can come inside while I fetch him."

"Thank you." Alex stepped onto the enclosed front porch being sure to wipe his feet. Then he took a seat at a table in the parlor while Pressley walked toward the back of the house. Alex could hear the tapping of typewriter keys in another room.

Soon Dr. Foreman entered the parlor bringing with him the fragrance of the cold outdoors. Without prelude, he said, "So let's have a look at that painting, young man," while he rubbed his hands to warm them.

Alex took out the painting and set it on the table. Foreman stepped back to admire it.

"This is truly remarkable," he enthused. "But are sure about selling it?"

"Yes, sir."

"Nettie won't serve us both up for lunch, will she?"

Alex smiled nervously. "I hope she'll understand."

The author nodded in a way that told Alex he understood. "It will be my pleasure to purchase it. How much do you want for it?"

"I hardly know how to price it, sir. I'm new to this."

"I'll give you $60 for it," Foreman said. "It's worth more than that but Carolyn won't let me go any higher than that."

"That's more than generous, sir." That would give him just enough extra money to buy a new canvas and art supplies for school.

Grant extended his hand and the two men shook on the deal. He walked to a little desk tucked in the corner of the room, opened a drawer and pulled out a checkbook.

"Will you take my personal check?"

"Yes, sir."

The author hastily scribbled the check details, signed it with a flourish and returned to the table to hand it to Alex.

The young man glanced at the check before slipping it into his pocket. He was happy and sad all at once so he kept picturing the antique earrings on his lovely wife and reminding himself that this was what she deserved.

Dr. Foreman lifted the painting from the table to look at it more closely.

"Come see what I just bought you," he called to his wife.

The typing in the other room stopped and soon Carolyn Foreman stepped into the room.

"What is it, dear?"

"A new painting," he responded, then made the introductions.

"Carolyn, this is Alex Barnett . . . Alex, my wife Carolyn."

Alex shook the hand the woman offered him then watched her reaction as she turned to study the painting. Her face said she was pleased with her gift.

"Is this the student A.C. told us about?" Mrs. Foreman asked her husband.

"Yes. He and Nettie Wheeler both think he's quite the up-and-comer."

"Well, I can certainly see why. You are quite talented, young man. This is beautiful." She smiled at Alex.

"Thank you. I'm glad you like it."

"Where shall we display it, dear," Mrs. Foreman then asked her husband. "Over the mantle, do you think?"

"I think I want it in my office," he replied. "I can be inspired by it while I'm writing."

"Very well," Carolyn smiled, "though you did say you bought it for me."

"I did, didn't I? Do you want it in your office?"

"No, mine is too small. We'll put it in yours."

The couple smiled at one another and Alex could tell that they had the kind of strong and lasting love he prayed he would always have with Laura.

Dr. Foreman extended his hand to Alex once again. "Thank you, Barnett, for letting me purchase this."

"I'm the one who must thank you," Alex countered. "I can now get a Christmas gift for my wife."

"Oh, lovely," Carolyn smiled, clasping her hands together. "Wish her a happy Christmas from us as well."

"I will," Alex promised, though he wasn't sure exactly when he would do so. Laura mustn't know he had come here to sell the painting until after he had presented her with the earrings. He knew she might be a little miffed at him when she learned what he had done, but he hoped she would understand why he had wanted so much to give her a very special gift. She had given everything for him . . . he wanted to do the same for her.

"Well, I must be going," Alex roused himself from his brief reverie and reached for the now-empty portfolio. "I wish you both a Merry Christmas and thank you again."

As if he had been waiting within hearing, Pressley entered the room and escorted Alex to the front door.

The artist walked casually down the front sidewalk but when he reached the street corner, he quickened his pace. He wanted to return the portfolio to the apartment, then hurry to McEntee's and buy the earrings before they were sold out from under him.

Only a half hour later, he entered the jewelry shop. Approaching the counter he saw that the same clerk he had asked to hold the earrings was trying to appear busy with a feather duster. There were no other customers in the shop.

"Hello," Alex greeted the man. "I have come for the earrings I asked you to hold for me."

The clerk made little attempt to hide his surprise.

"Of, course," he said. He laid down the duster and reached for the little jewelry box waiting under the counter. "Are you paying with cash?"

"Of course," Alex matched the man's tone. He found a great satisfaction in counting out the crisp bills he had received from the bank.

The man eyed the money suspiciously, but then swept up the bills and slipped them into the cash register.

"Do you gift wrap?" Alex asked him, wishing to get the full benefit of his hard-earned money.

"No," was the curt answer.

Alex shrugged. "Then Merry Christmas," he said with a smile. He took up the little box, opened it to check the earrings, then carefully slipped the gift into an inside pocket of his coat. He turned on his heel and left the shop, walking briskly toward home.

He hid the little box in the bottom of his sock drawer, wondering where he could get some wrapping paper or even just a bow for the gift. He would wait until Christmas Eve to place it under the popcorn-wrapped tree. He didn't want Laura to guess what he had purchased for her.

At the theater the next afternoon, he asked Charlie about wrapping paper. "Any ideas for wrapping a Christmas gift?" he asked.

"How big a gift?"

"The size of a jewelry box."

"You come into some money or something?" Charlie kidded his friend.

"I managed to find enough to get Laura something."

"What about the funny papers? That's what we use at our house sometimes."

"You mean from the newspaper?" Alex lifted an eyebrow. "No. That would never work."

"Oh, yeah," Charlie smiled ruefully. "I see what you mean. Laura doesn't allow her daddy's newspaper in your house?"

"No, she doesn't."

"Well, let me look around backstage. There's always leftover paper from this or that show. I can probably find something."

"Thanks, I appreciate it."

True to his word, Charlie found Alex before the doors were set to open for the evening movie – the latest one starring Shirley Temple.

"Will this work?" Charlie asked, holding up a bit of silver gauze.

"Yeah, thanks, I'll make it work," Alex replied while stuffing the fabric into his pocket. "You're sure this is just scrap I can use?"

"Oh, sure, there are all sorts of odds and ends just tossed into a corner."

"Great, I appreciate it."

The two young men went to their positions – Alex stationed at the theater doors, Charlie upstairs in the projection room. While the movie ran, Alex tried to imagine Laura opening the gift on Christmas morning. He knew she would be surprised; he hoped she would be pleased.

At the Art Shop the next day after work, Laura waited while Tom went to a back room to retrieve the frame. Alex was working late at the theater so she would be able to sneak the frame into the apartment without him seeing it.

She had thought about bringing the painting to Tom so he could put it in the frame, but didn't want to risk Alex checking on it in his portfolio. They could bring in the painting and frame for assembly after Christmas and still have plenty of time to deliver it to the art competition in Tulsa.

Tom appeared from the back, carrying the silvery-gray rectangle.

"You have something to wrap this in?" he asked as he set the large frame on the counter.

"Yes, Miss Wade at Calhoun's let me take some end pieces from rolls we use at the store. They're a little wrinkled, but I can iron them out and they'll work just fine."

"Good," Tom smiled. "Just bring it back with the painting whenever you're ready and I'll get it put together for your husband. I can't wait to hear how he does at this contest. You let me know if he wins, won't you."

"Yes, you'll be among the first to know. I can't thank you enough for your help."

"It's my pleasure. I'll be open tomorrow and Christmas Eve. If you need anything else, you stop in and see me. But if I don't see you, I hope you two have a Merry Christmas."

"Merry Christmas to you too," Laura smiled and left the shop feeling so happy with her purchase. Alex might not like the fact that she had sold her necklace, but he would surely be thrilled that this frame would enable him to enter the competition that she hoped would launch his career.

Before leaving Calhoun's, Laura had folded the wrapping paper and slipped it into her purse. She was glad the large frame wasn't yet wrapped for it would have been awkward and would have required two hands to carry it home otherwise.

Just to be safe, when she arrived at the apartment she set the gift in their landlady's garage, then went upstairs to make sure Alex was not home for some reason. Finding the apartment empty, she retrieved the frame and brought it into the kitchen setting it on the table.

She planned to heat up some soup for her supper and then get out the ironing board to smooth out the wrapping paper. Once the frame was wrapped, she would hide it behind the Christmas tree. She was glad for the tree's size for she knew Alex wouldn't see her gift to him until she brought it out. It would be quite obvious what was under the wrapping paper so she would keep it hidden until Christmas morning.

While she ate, Laura pondered whether she should try to wrap the painting with the frame. That way Alex could see immediately how wonderfully the frame complimented his work. But she wasn't sure she wanted to risk any damage to the painting. Remembering how carefully both Alex and Tom at the Art Shop had handled the art piece, she decided she wouldn't try to wrap it.

Laura rinsed out her soup bowl and tidied the kitchen a bit before pulling the ironing board out of the bedroom closet. Her eyes fell on the portfolio sitting in the corner. Alex had moved the scuffed case this morning to this place where it was less likely to be bumped. The young wife couldn't resist the temptation to hold the frame up to the painting to see again how perfectly suited they were to one another.

She brought the frame into the bedroom and set it on the bed. Then reaching for the portfolio, she was surprised at how light it felt. Carefully she set it on the bed and unzipped it slowly. She was even more surprised to find the case empty.

For several seconds Laura stared at the chamois cloth that had once wrapped the exquisite painting. She could not fathom why the painting was missing. She looked around the room and even under the bed. Their apartment was tiny with few places big enough to hide that painting. Remembering her plan, she even looked behind the Christmas tree. The painting was simply nowhere in their little abode.

Laura sank to the bed and stared at the empty portfolio. Surely they had not been robbed. Alex would have noticed if his artwork had not been in the case this morning and nothing had seemed amiss when Laura arrived home from work this afternoon. She glanced around the room. They had little worth stealing, but nothing else seemed to be missing.

What was going on here?

Then the horrible realization struck her.

"No, Alex," she whispered into the stark stillness. "You didn't sell it. Why would you do that?"

What was her stubborn husband thinking? And what good was a beautiful, expensive frame with no painting to embrace?

Laura felt sick to her stomach. She stared at the wooden frame and wanted to cry. Her special gift now seemed worthless.

Chapter 10

Alex noticed the next morning that today was the second time Laura had worn her white blouse without her grandmother's locket. He wondered if the clasp was broken and Laura didn't want to go to the expense of having it repaired.

He thought it would add a special touch to the gift of the earrings if he could fix the clasp. So when Laura left for work, Alex went to her jewelry case. He found it locked, but knew she kept the key in a drawer in the bureau. Locating it, he inserted it in the lock and the case sprang open.

He glanced through the box. Where was the necklace? This was where Laura always stored it because the lock kept it safe. And he was sure she had not been wearing it today.

Laura got into this case every morning for the few pieces of costume jewelry she wore for work. Surely she would have said something if the locket was missing.

He searched more carefully one more time. Lifting out the top tray, he saw what he had failed to notice before. The two heart-shaped photos she had always kept in the locket rested in the bottom of the box under a beaded bracelet.

Laura must have taken the pictures out of the locket, but why? What had she done with the necklace that meant so much to her?

"Cassie is always after her to sell it," Alex mused aloud. "I can't believe she would have done it though. She loves that locket. What would have caused her to sell it?"

He shook his head in dismay. His eyes fell on the portfolio in the corner. He had paid dearly for the perfect gift for Laura. But it was all for nothing. What good was a matching set of earrings with nothing to match?

That evening the couple ate their supper of leftovers in pensive silence. Both were absorbed in thoughts of Christmas morning and gifts that were now all wrong. They tried to disguise their thoughts and their sense of disappointment that such well-made plans had gone awry.

Finally when the meal was almost over, Laura raised her head and looked at Alex. "What are your work hours tomorrow?"

"I have to be at the theater at 10:00," he said. "There will be a children's matinee, then a visit from Santa Claus. Charlie tells me that afterwards, Mr. Procter has a little party for his employees and gives everyone a Christmas ham and some fruit and nuts. So we'll have a ham for Christmas dinner."

"That's awfully nice of him" Laura said. "So you'll be home around 2:00?"

"Yeah, that's probably right. There won't be an evening show. What about you? When will Calhoun's close for the day?"

"At noon. We'll probably be really busy with last minutes shoppers all morning so we're opening early again."

"So we can spend a quiet evening together."

"Yes," Laura smiled a sad tremulous smile. "That will be nice, won't it?"

"Yes." Alex stared at his plate. "Yes, it will."

Laura was re-arranging the perfume bottles at her counter the next morning when she saw her father enter the store. She felt surprise for she could never recall seeing him in Calhoun's at any time since she had started working here.

Then she remembered a joke she and her mother shared every Christmas. They had laughingly reminded each other to thank the salesclerk at whatever store their gift had come from that year. Sam Rigsby liked to buy nice gifts and he tried to patronize all the stores that bought advertising from him. But Laura and her mother had long ago realized that he never knew what to buy and so always asked the shop girls for help in choosing.

Of, course he has waited until the last minute, Laura thought. She kept her eyes on the products at her counter hoping he wouldn't see her or come her way. But very shortly, she felt his presence, smelled his musky cologne and knew it was his highly polished, expensive shoes standing in front of her.

She looked up at him, telling herself to be polite and professional. She could not make a scene in the store. Whatever snide remark he might make about Alex, she would simply ignore.

"Hello, Laura." His voice was quiet, even conciliatory. Perhaps Mother had sent him to apologize.

"Hello, Daddy. Can I help you with something?"

"What would your mother like? You know her tastes so well."

"She likes Dior." Laura reached for one of the small and most expensive bottles kept in the glass case below the counter. "Would you like to smell it?" she offered, taking up one of the pretty pink sample papers.

"No, I don't need to. I trust your judgment."

"Do you?" Her voice challenged his comment. He had done nothing but question her judgment since he found out she was dating a boy from the other side of town.

But as soon as her words were out of her mouth Laura wanted to take back them back. She was not going to get into another argument with her father. Miss Wade would likely fire her if she did.

"I trust you in this, certainly. And in other things."

"Other things?"

Rigsby sighed. "I didn't mean to hurt you, dear. I hope you know that. I just thought . . ."

"You thought I could do better," Laura finished his statement. "Well, I couldn't have, Daddy. Alex is a wonderful husband and a wonderful artist. You're going to see that someday."

Sam Rigsby looked down at his well-manicured hand. "George Procter seems to think he's good."

"So does Nettie Wheeler at the Sugar Bowl."

"Yes, I understand she has some competition for him to enter."

Laura felt a knife in her heart. "Well, I don't know if that's going to happen." She hated having to admit that to her father.

"Why not?"

"There's some cost involved." Laura would not go into all the details of her failed attempt to help with that issue.

"I see." Rigsby kept his voice cool and Laura could tell that he too was trying not to argue or say something else he might regret. He waved a hand at the perfume Laura still held.

"Can you wrap that for me?"

"Certainly." Laura knew their exchange was over. She pulled out a box and a couple of different styles of wrapping paper. After her father chose one, she wrapped the perfume and placed it in a little holiday bag. He paid the princely sum, they exchanged polite thanks and then her father walked out of the department store.

Laura watched him go, blinking back bitter tears. She glanced at the clock hanging at the back of the store. Just a half hour until closing and she could leave. She would count down the minutes.

Chapter 11

Christmas morning dawned frosty bright and clear. Two gifts waited under the tree – one small and the other quite large.

Alex and Laura said good morning under a little sprig of mistletoe hung at the bedroom door. It would just be the two of them here alone for Christmas with the smell of cedar mixing with that of an apple butter glazed ham cooking in the oven. After breakfast, they settled on the floor in front of the tree with hot cocoa, created from the chocolates in Mr. Procter's gift box.

"You go first," Laura told Alex after they both had eyed the gifts that awaited them for a long minute.

"No, you," Alex countered.

"I insist," Laura said, reaching for the large rectangle. She handed it to Alex. He set down his mug to accept it.

This was the first he had seen it and he briefly wondered how Laura had kept it hidden until this morning.

"It was behind the tree," Laura smiled, able to read his questioning thoughts.

The gift Alex held was exactly the size of . . . .

"Laura, you didn't," he said, realization dawning on his face.

"You needed a frame for your painting," Laura explained.

Alex swallowed hard. "Laura, I sold the painting," he whispered apologetically.

"I know."

"You know?"

"Just open it."

Carefully, Alex pulled at the tape on the package. Laura had a surprisingly happy look on her face considering he had just confessed to selling the art piece she had purchased a frame for. He finally freed one end of the wrapping and reach in to pull out its contents. Instead of a frame, the "Star That Travels" painting came out into his hands.

His mouth fell open. "Laura!" he exclaimed. "How did you . . .? When did you . . ?" He was so shocked he couldn't even form words.

"I couldn't let you sell your painting yet, Alex. That competition is too important for your career."

"But how? How did you know who had bought it?"

"I remembered that Dr. Foreman had offered to buy it so I called him after work yesterday. He and his wife were so kind. They let me buy it back."

"How could you afford it?"

"I took the frame I had bought back to the Art Shop, got my money back, then bought the painting."

"But a frame . . . I've priced those things. They're not cheap. How could you afford . . . oh, that's why you sold your locket."

"My locket?" Now it was Laura's turn to be surprised. "You know about the locket?"

"I sold the painting to buy you those antique earrings at McEntee's to match it," Alex explained as he handed Laura the other gift under the tree. "I knew you wanted them, but would never ask. They match the necklace perfectly."

"Oh, Alex, you shouldn't have," Laura was saying as she tore the silver fabric off with trembling fingers. She opened the black velvet case slowly. Nestled in the folds of the cloth inside was the heart-shaped locket.

"Grandmother's necklace!" she exclaimed, throwing herself into Alex's arms. "How did you find it?"

"I checked with Cassie yesterday," he laughed, folding his arms around her. "She'd decided to hold it for awhile in case you changed your mind."

"Bless Cassie," Laura said. She carefully pulled out the locket and opened it. "You put the pictures back. Good."

"I hope I'm never out of your heart," Alex said tenderly.

"You never will be," Laura promised, looking into his eyes.

They shared a deep and lasting kiss. Then they settled back against the sofa with Laura snuggled in her husband's arms. They looked with satisfaction at the two gifts they had given one another.

For a time they were lost in quiet thought, only the hiss of the radiator breaking the peaceful silence. Then they roused themselves and went to the kitchen to work on dinner preparations.

To their surprise a knock sounded at the door.

"Who could that be?" Laura asked as she tied on her apron. "I wasn't expecting anyone, were you?"

"No," Alex said as he crossed to the door. "Maybe Santa forgot to leave us something," he joked.

He opened the door to find his friend Charlie standing outside, wearing a Santa hat and holding a large wrapped gift.

"It is Santa," Alex laughed.

"Hey, Charlie," Laura came to greet him. "Come on in."

Charlie stepped inside out of the cold and Alex closed the door.

"I can't stay long," he explained. "Aunt Eudora's cooking for the whole clan and I have to get back before I'm missed. I'm just running this errand for Mr. Procter."

"Mr. Procter?"

"Yeah," Charlie explained as he handed the large rectangle to Alex. "I was helping clean up after the party yesterday and he asked me to stop at his office before I left. When I went up there, Lillian gave me this and said I was to bring it to you today."

Alex exchanged a puzzled look with Laura.

"Well, open it," she said.

Taking less care than he had with his wife's gift, Alex tore off the wrapping.

Laura gasped when she saw what was revealed. The frame – the exact one Tom had chosen -- was now in Alex's hand.

"How did Mr. Procter know? Did he buy this?"

"I don't know who bought it," Charlie responded. "The way Lillian talked it was someone else, but she didn't say who it was."

"Maybe Miss Wheeler?" Alex suggested.

"Maybe Dr. Foreman?" Laura said. She picked up the wrapping paper to see if there was a gift tag on it. There was nothing, either inside or out. But she caught a distinctive scent of musky cologne.

"Daddy!" she whispered in shock. She covered her mouth as tears began to form. "I think it's from Daddy."

"How would he know that I needed a frame?" Alex puzzled. "You didn't ask him, did you, Laura? We promised we wouldn't."

"No, I didn't ask. But he was at Calhoun's yesterday to buy a gift for Mother. He knew about the competition from Mr. Procter. Maybe they decided to do something together. If they had talked to Miss Wheeler or checked with Tom at the Art Shop, they would have known you needed a frame."

"I can't accept this from your father."

"Clearly Daddy didn't want us to know it was from him. I think he's trying to make amends, Alex. I think he realizes he was wrong and this is his way of showing it."

"I don't want your father's charity."

"Seems like this is a Christmas gift, Alex," Charlie interjected. "Would you accept a gift from Mr. Procter or Miss Wheeler? You accepted that ham baking in the oven."

Alex seemed torn as he looked at Charlie and then Laura. He battled with pride but in the end settled on practicality. With a sigh, he said, "All right, I'll accept it."

"Yea," Laura clapped her hands and hugged him around the frame he still held.

"Well, now that that's settled, I need to get back home," Charlie grinned. He slipped out the door while Alex took the frame to the living room. Laura returned to the kitchen to finish dinner preparations.

They enjoyed their meal of ham with potatoes and red-eyed gravy, corn casserole and sweet potato pie. After the dishes had been washed, they returned to the living room and enjoyed listening to records on an old Victrola phonograph.

Snuggling on the sofa, they admired a soft snowfall that had begun in the late afternoon. They also admired the painting, now propped against the wall with the frame around it.

"Tom did a good job in selecting that frame," Alex commented.

"Yes, he did. It just sets off the colors perfectly. I know the judges are going to love it."

"Remember the story behind this painting?" Alex asked after a moment.

"Your great-grandfather chose his adult name as Star-That-Travels because of the Christmas story. Wasn't that it?"

"Yes, but that is not all. He had spent the night alone on the prairie before his naming ceremony. He tried to count the stars to stay awake. He had heard a priest tell the Christmas story, but he found the idea of a star traveling across the sky implausible. Then as he watched the stars, he saw some of them begin to fall, streaking across the sky."

"It was a meteor shower?"

"Probably. But he was young and had never seen such a thing before. He took it as a sign that the story the priest told him was true and he believed."

"I remember you telling that now. And he went to the priest to tell him what had happened."

"Yes, and Grandfather asked the minister what gift he could give the Child just as the Magi had."

Alex paused as he tried to remember the details of the story long passed down in his family.

"The priest told my great-grandfather to give himself, for that was the only thing that the Lord didn't have and was the one thing he wanted most in the world. So that's what Stat-That-Travels gave him."

"A greater gift than the gift of the Magi," Laura mused. "The perfect gift is giving yourself."

Alex nodded and pressed a kiss against her cheek. "You, sweet Laura, are my perfect gift."

"And you are mine."

Other Books by Jonita Mullins

Historical Fiction
The Missions of Indian Territory
1. Journey to an Untamed Land
2. Look Unto the Fields
3. Come to Lovely County

The Neosho District
1. The Marital Scandal

Love's Perfect Gift

Historical Non-Fiction
Haskell
Glimpses of Our Past
Life Along the Rivers
The Jefferson Highway in Oklahoma
Oklahoma Originals

Others
A Kitchen on the Frontier
Making a Point
The Whatsoever Things

Sign up for Jonita's newsletter at her website: okieheritage.com.